There was a long moment when they were still. When anything was possible.

Abbey took a shaken breath, tilting her face up to his, thinking she should stop this now. But the urge to touch him and to be touched in return was too great. Suddenly all her senses began to stir, unfold, waken. Her heart did a back-flip in her chest. And she was waiting, expectant, when Nick leaned forward to claim her mouth…

DOCTORS DOWN UNDER

In Medical Romance™ you'll find a special kind of doctor. Flying doctors, bush doctors, family doctors and city specialists from Sydney, Brisbane or Auckland. Whether they're battling with life and love decisions in the hot and harsh locations of the wilderness or dealing with the personal and medical dramas of city life, they exude a determination, dedication and an earthy charm that only comes from Down Under.

DOCTORS DOWN UNDER

They're irresistible

From Mills & Boon® Medical Romance™

OUTBACK SURGEON

BY
LEAH MARTYN

MILLS & BOON

For Hilary, who knows the journey.

*First published in Great Britain 2003
Large Print edition 2004
Harlequin Mills & Boon Limited,
Eton House, 18-24 Paradise Road,
Richmond, Surrey TW9 1SR*

© Leah Martyn 2003

ISBN 0 263 18132 4

*Set in Times Roman 16½ on 18½ pt.
17-0104-45591*

*Printed and bound in Great Britain
by Antony Rowe Ltd, Chippenham, Wiltshire*

CHAPTER ONE

'THANKS, guys. That was terrific!'

Off camera, the television producer favoured his guests with a satisfied grin, his gaze lingering with obvious approval on the female of the pair, Dr Abbey Jones.

Abbey dredged up a dry smile. 'I'm always happy to comment on rural health matters, Rob. You know that. But next time, warn me if I'm here for a debate, will you?' Lifting her chin, she sent a cool, tawny look at her opponent in the debate, Dr Nicholas Tonnelli.

Tonnelli's mouth quirked in a smile that just missed being patronising and she practically had to force herself to accept the hand he extended to formally end their debate.

'You presented an irresistible challenge, Dr Jones.'

Abbey took a shallow breath as her hand vanished inside his. His touch was warm and

5

dry and his green eyes gleamed down at her. 'I enjoyed our encounter,' he added softly.

Disconcerted, she reclaimed her hand as though she feared being burned by the impact, turning away to gather up her hastily scribbled notes. Her lungs heaved in a controlling breath. Her hands, with a mind of their own, began shoving the A4 pages awkwardly into her briefcase.

Chewing her bottom lip, Abbey reluctantly admitted that Tonnelli had been a formidable opponent, his skilled ad lib presentation spurring her on to try to salvage something even halfway credible for her side of the argument.

And it had hardly been fair of Rob, she remonstrated silently, pitting her, a rural GP, against one of Sydney's up and coming spinal surgeons.

Physically, he hadn't been what she'd expected either. But, then, what had she expected? Occasionally, when she'd flipped through the Sydney newspapers, she'd glimpsed pictures of him in the social pages. But now, having met him in the flesh, she had to admit that the black and white images hadn't done him justice. They'd certainly given no indication of the man's almost tangible charisma.

She caught back a huff of irritation. Perhaps he'd won the debate, perhaps he hadn't. But whatever the TV ratings showed, she'd just bet his high-voltage sexy smile had sizzled all the way to the female viewers' little hearts.

But not to hers. Heavens, she wasn't that easily taken in!

A glance at her watch told her she'd have to forego the coffee and cake Rob usually offered and make a quick exit from the studio.

'I'm just off, Rob.' Her professional smile in place, Abbey looked to where the two males were seemingly in close private conversation beside the now-darkened set.

'Already?' Rob Stanton turned, taking several quick strides towards her. 'Thanks again, Abbey, for making yourself available at such short notice. You saved my bacon.'

A chink of wry humour lit her smile. 'A nice fat donation to our hospital funds should be in order, then.'

'Hey, you've got it!' Rob was enthusiastic, as though he'd thought of the idea himself. 'I'll OK it right away.'

'Thanks,' Abbey murmured and shot a level look at Tonnelli. 'Goodbye, Doctor.' She began to turn away and then took a quick breath, her senses clanging when the surgeon moved fast enough to block her way as she made to go past him.

'Do you have to rush off, Dr Jones?'

Abbey glared at him, realising belatedly that now they were not seated, she had to raise her gaze a good six inches to meet his eyes. 'Yes, I do.'

'Let me buy you lunch.'

'No, thank you.'

'What've I done?' The charismatic, mocking face was close to hers and she felt every nerve in her body contract. His mouth, wearing its sexy smile, was getting close to hers, so close she could feel the warm whisper of his breath, take in the clean smell of sandalwood soap on his skin.

Get out of my space, she wanted to tell him calmly and coolly. Instead, she felt her insides grind painfully, as she took an uncertain step backwards, rocking a little on her high heels. 'If you don't mind, Dr Tonnelli, I have a tight schedule today. I just want to get on with my own business.'

'Oh, come on, Doctor… We're off camera now. Can't we bury the hatchet?' he asked, his tone almost an amused drawl.

Abbey tried to fix him with a steely glare and failed miserably. 'I don't have time to sit around having long lunches, Dr Tonnelli.'

He lifted a shoulder dismissively. 'It needn't necessarily be a long lunch. I know a place where the service is fast and the food actually pretty good.'

'McDonald's?' Abbey parried innocently.

His mouth gave the merest twist of a smile. 'A little more upmarket. Margo's. Heard of it?'

'No.'

When she still hesitated, he added persuasively, 'Surely you usually eat something before you head off on that long drive back to Wingara?'

'I *usually* just grab a sandwich or some fruit to eat in the car.' Abbey began to feel pushed into a corner, almost mesmerised by the subtle challenge in his eyes. And they couldn't stand here much longer. The TV crew packing up their gear were beginning to latch onto the possibility of some gossip. 'Oh, all right, then,' she said, uncomfortably aware her acceptance sounded ungracious, explaining, 'I've a dozen things still to do and a patient to see at Sunningdale rehab centre before I head back west, so I'll need to keep it short, OK?'

'Deal.' He looked pleased. Or rewarded, Abbey thought waspishly, watching him. 'Did you come by cab?' he asked.

Oh, for heaven's sake! Who could afford cabs any more? 'I drove my own vehicle. I'm parked outside.'

'Me too.' Moving smoothly away from her, he opened the heavy glass door to the foyer.

This is crazy, Abbey fretted, her heart fluttering like the wings of a trapped bird as they made their way past the flowering shrubs to the car park. And why did it have to be *him* she'd had to cross swords with and ruin her day? There were any number of registrars at the district hospital Rob could have approached to fill the gap. But, then, they wouldn't have had the impact of Tonnelli.

She sighed and brought her head up, her fair silky bob sliding back from her cheekbones, her thoughts still on the surgeon. It was rumoured in medical circles that he was a genius at just about anything he turned his mind to. A man firmly at the centre of his own universe.

Not to mention his reputation with women…

Well, I don't want him propositioning *me,* she decided through gritted teeth, coming to a stop beside the door of her maroon Range Rover. 'This is me.' Her shoulder brushed against his upper arm, and she found herself staring into his eyes. And taking a sharp little breath. His eyes had the luminosity of an early-morning ocean, she thought fancifully. A kind of wintergreen…

'I'm over there.'

She blinked, following the backward flex of his thumb to the metallic grey Jaguar. It suits him, she decided, having no trouble at all personifying the car's sleek elegance and controlled power and making the comparison with its owner.

'It's probably best if you follow me.' He looked at her from under slightly lowered lids. 'Margo's is rather tucked away, an old house that's been refurbished into a restaurant. But I'm afraid the parking's non-existent—just stop along the street, wherever you can.' He raised the briefest smile. 'See you there in a bit.'

Abbey nodded assent, climbing into her vehicle, tapping her fingers impatiently on the steering-wheel, her gaze following his tall, lithe figure as he strode towards his vehicle on the periphery of the car park.

Her wide, sensitive mouth with its gloss of soft coral firmed into a moue of conjecture. Just what was Nicholas Tonnelli doing here in Hopeton anyway? As far as she knew he didn't operate anywhere outside his own hospital, St Thomas's in Sydney's rather affluent North Shore area. So what had brought him here to a small provincial city in the Central West of New South Wales in the middle of a working week?

He'd almost blown it.

Nick Tonnelli wondered why he'd pushed her so hard. 'Male ego at its worst,' he muttered, grimacing with self-derision, groping in the glove box for his sunglasses. But she *had* accepted his invitation, hadn't she? Yeah, right! Reluctantly, mate. Get real.

A tight little smile drifted around his mouth. Who'd have thought spending a couple of days R and R in his home town and doing a favour for his mate, Rob Stanton, would have led to his meeting someone like the feisty, quite delectable Dr Abbey Jones?

The lady was like a breath of sweet, clean air. And he'd become so bored with the Sydney social scene lately. So utterly, utterly bored.

*   *   *

Abbey glanced across the car park once more. At last! Tonnelli was in motion. In a kind of sick anticipation, she lowered her hand to the ignition switch, her mind simultaneously ago-nising over what on earth they'd find to talk about over lunch.

Alternatively, she supposed she could save herself the grief and lose him deliberately on the way to the restaurant... A jagged laugh caught in her throat at the very idea.

The journey to Margo's was completed quite quickly, with Abbey keeping Tonnelli's distinctive vehicle in sight as she followed him in and out of several back streets, until he in-dicated he was about to stop and she glanced sideways and saw the restaurant's sign.

She looked in vain for a parking spot and ended up having to drive further along the nar-row street, scattering tiny bits of gravel, when she finally ground her four-wheel-drive to a halt.

Tonnelli gave her an apologetic half-smile when she joined him outside the restaurant. 'The food will more than compensate for the parking hassles,' he promised, guiding her along the flagstone path to the entrance.

Although it was just on midday, the place was already filled with the hushed sounds of patrons dining—a muted hum of conversation, the soft clink of cutlery on china—and an absolutely delicious aroma wafting from the kitchen.

'Oh, it's lovely!' Abbey's comment was spontaneous. Entranced, she looked around her at the walls, papered with a country-style pattern of meadowsweet flowers, and at the framed prints, each one essentially outback Australian, depicting the lifestyles of its drovers, ringers and stockmen.

Told you so, Tonnelli's little nod of satisfaction seemed to imply. 'It's a blackboard menu.' His dark head was turned attentively towards her. 'We'll order first and then with a bit of luck we'll find a table.' His green gaze swept over the precincts. 'It's crowded today. The livestock sales must be on in town.' He considered the blackboard. 'Ah, it's Italian today. Fancy some pasta?'

Abbey's teeth caught on her lower lip. 'I think I'll just have the house salad, thanks.'

'OK.' Nick Tonnelli tapped his fingers on the polished countertop, considering his own choice. 'But you must try one of their stuffed potatoes,' he insisted. 'And the home-made bread.'

Abbey spread her hands helplessly. 'You must think I need fattening up.'

'Hardly.' His eyes softened for a moment. 'I'd say the packaging is perfect as it is.' He added a slow, very sweet smile then, and it was as though his fingers played over her skin.

For a split second Abbey registered a riveting awareness between them. Raw and immediate. Like an electric current and just as tangible. She swallowed thickly. 'I'll, um, freshen up while you order, then.'

'Will you have something to drink?' He detained her with the lightest touch to her forearm. 'White wine, perhaps?'

Abbey considered her options swiftly. 'A mineral water, I think. I've a long drive ahead of me.'

'We'll meet at the bar, then.' Two little lines appeared between his dark brows. 'Don't do a runner on me, will you?'

Abbey felt the heat warm her cheeks as she spun away. How had he guessed she'd actually considered it? Perhaps he read minds along with his other talents, she thought cynically.

In the restroom, she did a quick make-up repair. Taking out her small cosmetic bag, she freshened her lipstick, swiped a comb through her hair and added a squirt of her favourite cologne.

In the mirror with its lovely old-fashioned gilded frame, she looked critically at her reflection, unnerved to see a flush in her cheeks she hadn't seen there in ages.

She was suddenly conscious of her stomach churning. She must have been crazy to have agreed to this lunch, she berated herself for the umpteenth time. She and Tonnelli had nothing in common. For starters, their lifestyles had to be poles apart.

As a senior surgeon in a state-of-the-art hospital, he could have no concept of her world, she reflected thinly. Her little hospital at Wingara was reasonably well equipped, mostly due to the tireless money-raising efforts of the locals. But even so it had to be light years away from what she imagined as Tonnelli's clinical environment.

She hitched up her shoulder-bag, her mind throwing up yet again the question of what on earth would they find to talk about. Heart thrumming, she left the restroom and began making her way back to the bar. She saw him at once, his distinctive dark head with its short cut turning automatically, almost as if he'd sensed her approach. 'Thanks.' Abbey took the drink he handed to her.

'I believe there's a table for us in the garden room.' He began leading the way towards the rear of the restaurant to a cleverly conceived extension like a conservatory, complete with glass walls and ceiling.

He saw her comfortably seated and Abbey took a moment to look around her. Their table was set with crisp, palest cream linen, gleaming silver and glassware, and decorating the centre was a trailing arrangement of multicoloured garden flowers. She felt her spirits lift and decided to make a huge effort. 'I'm actually looking forward to our lunch.'

'Much better than a sandwich from the deli,' he agreed. 'Cheers.' Lifting his glass of ice-cold lager, he took a mouthful. 'I asked for our peasant bread to be brought first. I don't know about you, but I'm starving.'

Even as he finished speaking, a smiling waitress placed the still-warm loaf on the table with the accompanying little pats of butter.

Abbey eyed the crusty, flour-dusted high round loaf hungrily, feeling her digestive juices begin to react.

'This looks good, hmm?' Without hesitation, Nick Tonnelli took up the breadknife, wielding it with surgical precision, separating the loaf quickly and efficiently into easily manageable portions.

Watching him, Abbey said faintly, 'You must be a whiz with the Sunday roast, Dr Tonnelli.'

'Each to his own talent, Abbey,' he responded blandly. 'And for crying out loud, call me Nick.'

'Tell me about your patient in the rehab centre.' Nick Tonnelli's tone was suddenly professional and brisk.

Startled, Abbey looked up from her plate. Was he just being the polite host? she wondered. Pretending an interest? Making conversation for the sake of it? Whatever he was doing, she could hardly ignore such a pointed demand.

'His name is Todd Jensen. He's a twenty-five-year-old professional rodeo rider.' She looked bleak for a moment. 'Although I probably should be using the past tense here. It's almost certain we won't see him back on the rodeo circuit again.'

Nick's dark brows rose. 'What was it, a workplace accident of some kind?'

'Todd was participating in a buckjumping event. His mount threw him and in its panic struck him on the lower back with its hind hooves.'

The consultant winced and murmured a commiseration.

'It was a dreadful afternoon,' Abbey said quietly. 'Everyone was so shocked. Fortunately, the CareFlight chopper was on standby. Todd was flown straight here to Hopeton.'

Nick's mouth compressed. 'What did the MRI show? That's assuming he had one?'

'Of course he did.' Abbey resented his inference that Todd had somehow received second-class medical attention.

'The new scanning devices for magnetic resonance imaging are ruinously expensive,' Nick clarified. 'I merely wondered whether the district hospital here had managed to install one.'

'They have,' Abbey conceded guardedly. 'Mostly due to the efforts of Jack O'Neal and his committee.'

Nick rubbed a hand around his jaw. 'He's the SR on Kids', isn't he?'

Abbey nodded. 'Jack and his wife, Geena, are tireless fundraisers for the hospital.'

'Commendable.'

'Essential, seeing the shortfall in funding for rural hospitals.'

Nick acknowledged her comment politely. 'To get back to your patient. What did the MRI show?'

'Irreversible nerve damage.'

Nick frowned. 'So, what's his prognosis?'

Biting her lower lip, not sure where they were going with this, Abbey elaborated, 'A wheelchair existence. His accident placed a cloud over our whole community. Todd was well liked, a kind of icon to the young kids. And very good at what he did. The really sad part is he'd had an invitation from one of the rodeo associations in the States. He was about to take off and try his luck in the big time.'

She ran the pad of her thumb across the raised pattern of her glass. 'He's still so angry. Just recently, he told his wife to go and make a new life for herself—that he was only half a man…'

'So he's dropped the ball. That's a fairly normal reaction, Abbey,' Nick pointed out reasonably. 'At the moment his feelings have to be loaded with issues of masculinity and virility so, of course, he's told his wife to get lost. What's more to the point is what's being done presently for your patient? For starters, is his medication up to scratch? How intense is his physio programme? Has there been input from a psychologist? An occupational therapist?'

Abbey lifted her head and regarded him warily. He seemed in his element, rapping out questions. While she, on the other hand, felt as though she were under the microscope, almost an intern again being put through a consultant's wringer.

The silence stretched for a tense moment, until Abbey responded steadily, 'Todd's programme is as good as Sunningdale can provide. And distance-wise, it suits his family to have him there. At least they can make the three-hour drive once a week to see him. But realistically, I'd guess, he's gone about as far as he can go there. Sunningdale will want to discharge him soon.'

'And then what?'

Abbey frowned. 'Well, at this stage his parents are proposing to have him back home with them.'

'In the bush?'

She tilted her chin defensively. 'That's where they live.'

Nick made an impatient sound. 'What's he going to do there, cut wood for the fire from his wheelchair?' The surgeon shook his head. 'Surely we can do better than that, Abbey? Have you heard of the Dennison Foundation in Sydney?'

Abbey frowned. 'It's a fairly recent concept, isn't it?'

'State of the art in every way. Structured specifically for spinal rehab, with patients being taught how to accustom themselves to the physical realities of being disabled in an able-bodied world. I'm sure you'd see a great improvement in your Todd's ability to cope after a stay there. I'd refer him urgently, if I were you.'

A flush of annoyance rose in Abbey's cheeks. 'Ever heard of waiting lists, Doctor? Besides, his family couldn't afford those kinds of fees. And I can't imagine the management would be prepared to cut a special deal on a rural GP's referral.'

'What if I referred him?'

Something like resentment stirred in Abbey and she couldn't let go of it. 'Why should you bother? Todd's nothing to you.'

Nick Tonnelli's expression closed abruptly. 'As professionals, isn't it up to all of us who go under the guise of medical practitioners to assist all humankind where we can? So, Doctor, I suggest you pocket your false pride and face the facts as we have them.

'I'm willing to carry out a reassessment on your patient. Like Todd, I'm good at what I do. Maybe I can help him further. Maybe I can't. But I'm willing to try and if you think my name will help, I'll refer him to the

Dennison, if I deem it appropriate. It's up to you.'

Abbey clenched her hands on her lap and stared at them fiercely. He'd given her a terrible dressing-down. All done so quietly and lethally. Dear God! How she would hate to have to work with the man! Thoughts, none of them pleasant, crowded in on her. She should *never* have agreed to this lunch. She should have quit while she was ahead and left him standing in the car park, watching her dust.

She took a deep breath and tried to leave personal issues out of it. Todd's youthful face, stark with hope one minute and dark with despair the next, impinged on her vision. Much as she hated to admit it, Tonnelli was right. Pride had no place here. She would swallow hers, no matter how galling it might be, and ask for his help.

'When could you see Todd?' she asked hesitantly. 'I mean... I don't know your movements... If you have other commitments here...' She broke off helplessly.

He bit into his bread, his even white teeth leaving a neat half-circle. 'We could start the ball rolling after our lunch, if that suits you.'

'Fine.' Abbey teased at her lip. She should have known that once the decision was made, he'd want to sweep ahead.

'I would prefer to keep my involvement quite informal, if you don't mind,' he said easily. 'I'll need some time to study Todd's case details and speak with the staff, his physio and OT in particular.

'If I decide the programme at the Dennison will benefit Todd, I'll speak personally with the director, Anna Charles.' At once his expression lightened. 'We trained together. She's done extensive post-grad work at Harvard. A brilliant practitioner. Todd couldn't be in better hands.'

Abbey blinked uncertainly. 'And would she take him—just like that?'

'As a favour to me? Yes, she would.' He smiled, a mere sensual curving of his lips.

Abbey felt her cheeks burn as the possible meaning behind his remark occurred to her.

She pulled in a shattered breath. Forget Tonnelli and his women and think of Todd, she told herself with quiet desperation. 'What about the fees?'

Nick lifted a dismissive shoulder. 'I'll arrange something. Nothing in this life is set in concrete, Abbey. Nothing at all.'

CHAPTER TWO

THE main part of their meal was served just after Abbey's capitulation. She looked down at the appetising char-grilled strips of chicken, the crisp salad and accompanying stuffed potato, and despaired.

After the last few minutes, the tense trading of words with Nick Tonnelli, her throat seemed closed, her stomach knotted.

He, on the other hand, she noticed with faint irony, seemed not be suffering any repercussions at all. And after the first few uncomfortable minutes, after which he obviously set out to charm the socks off her, she felt a lessening of tension.

'So, Abbey, what do you do for relaxation at Wingara?' he asked, as they sat over their coffee later. 'No chance of snow sports, I expect?' he added with a touch of humour.

'Hardly.' She laughed, activating the tiny dimple in her cheek. 'I play tennis when I can and we have a sports centre with a pool and quite an active Little Theatre. And I have friends there now, good friends. One couple in particular, Stuart and Andrea Fraser, have quite a large property so I'm able to spend the odd weekend there, picnicking and so on.'

'So, no regrets about opting out of city mainstream medicine, then?' he teased gently, fixing her with his keen, gemstone gaze.

'Often,' Abbey rebuffed him sharply.

He blinked, appearing a little surprised by her answer. 'In what way?'

She lifted a shoulder. 'Broadly speaking, I could give you a dozen examples. But the bottom line is all I can do in a major medical emergency is to stabilise my patient and have them airlifted to the nearest major hospital. And just hope they survive the journey.'

'So what are you saying?' Nick's eyes took on a steely glint.

'Nothing I didn't say in the debate,' Abbey responded bluntly. 'That if a specialist surgeon could be on call to come to us, it would halve the trauma for both patient and family. And would, I dare say, be more cost-effective.'

'Bunkum!' Nick's hand cut the air dismissively. 'Logistics for one thing. Our rural population is so scattered, our distances so vast. All things considered, I believe we, as specialists, do a reasonable job.'

Abbey tossed her head up, throwing into sharp relief the long silky lashes framing the haunting beauty of her tawny eyes. 'When was the last time you conducted a clinic outside St Thomas's, then?'

With a reflex reaction Nick's head shot up, his green gaze striking an arc across the space between them. 'I've considered it but so far the consensus seems to be that it's more appropriate for the patients to come to me than vice versa.' In an abrupt movement, he dipped his head and pulled back the sleeve of his pale blue shirt. His mouth compressed briefly. 'If you've quite finished your coffee, we should be moving, I think.'

So, end of discussion. Abbey curled her mouth into a cynical little moue, bending to retrieve her shoulder-bag from the carpeted floor near her feet. Had she really expected the conversation to go any other way?

While Nick settled the bill, she made her way slowly outside, annoyance with herself shifting and compressing against her ribcage. It wouldn't do to get the man offside. Not now, when it seemed they were about to become involved professionally with Todd's care.

Beside her, a butterfly scooped the air, darting in and out of a border of cornflowers, its pale yellow wings a gauzy haze against the deep blue petals. Her shoulders lifted as she took a calming breath, belatedly registering the near-perfection of the afternoon—the crisp air, the softly falling leaves, the sky an unbroken bowl of china blue...

'Wonderful day.' From behind, Nick softly echoed her thoughts.

Startled, Abbey jerked back. How long had he been standing there? 'I love autumn.' She rushed into speech, embarrassed to be caught mooning like a teenager. 'Especially in this part of the state where the seasons are so clearly defined.'

'Perhaps.' Nick looked unconvinced but he was smiling. 'I still think I prefer the coast. I can well do without all this.' He scuffed a gathering pile of fallen leaves with his shoe.

'Didn't you have fun running through them when you were a kid, though?'

His head went back on a laugh. 'You know, I'd forgotten all that.'

Abbey listened to the small talk threading between them like a line of careful stitches, but at the same time acknowledging she'd have to upset the pattern and get things rather more settled in her own mind. 'Dr Tonnelli— Nick...' she began awkwardly, 'I hope you didn't feel obligated to get involved with my patient...'

Nick's gut tightened. She looked so uncertain, so vulnerable, he wanted to just to hold her, reassure her. Instead, he shoved his hands into the pockets of his trousers out of temptation's way. 'Abbey, I want to do it, OK?'

Her lips parted on a shaky breath. 'Are you sure?'

'I'm sure.' He permitted himself the ghost of a wry smile. 'Actually, it occurs to me I might have seemed to have taken over in there, come on a bit strong about your management of Todd. If I did, I apologise.'

Abbey's senses tightened and she felt confused at the odd mix of reactions chasing around inside her. 'Honestly, you don't need to.'

'Oh, I think I do.' He gave a taut smile. 'I stormed all over you. But, then, I have been accused of being arrogant once or twice. And what's the expression? If you have to eat crow, it's better to do it while it's still warm.'

Abbey smothered a laugh. 'Consider the crow eaten, then.'

She was thoughtful as they made their way down the path to the street. She guessed it had cost him something to have placed a question mark over his earlier behaviour.

But on the other hand, to have put her on the defensive the way he had had probably been nothing more than a normal reaction from him. Everything about the man indicated a natural authority, an obvious ability to give orders and have them carried out without question. There was no doubt about it, Nick Tonnelli was a man of substance and of power.

She stifled a sigh, seeing the stream of professional differences between them widen to a river.

'My time is my own but does it suit you to go across to Sunningdale now?' he was asking.

She nodded, grateful for his courtesy. 'I'll introduce you and stay for a quick visit with Todd. Then I'm afraid I'll have to leave. I've to go and plead for some lab reports I'm waiting on to be rushed through and collect a package of drugs from the pharmacy— What's that noise?' Suddenly, she turned her head up, listening.

Nick frowned. 'I don't— Ah! Motorbike by the sound of it.' Instinctively, he stiffened, stepping in front of Abbey as if to shield her. 'And going way too fast for a built-up area. Hell's bells!' he gasped as the high-pitched roar cut the still of the afternoon and a big black machine shot into view at the top of the street.

'Oh, lord!' Abbey watched in stark disbelief. 'The intersection's too narrow—he'll never take the corner! Nick...' Horrified, she grabbed the surgeon's arm as the bike became airborne.

Nick reacted like quicksilver. 'My car's closer—get my bag!' Wresting his keys from his side pocket, he slapped them into Abbey's hand. 'In the boot—go!' He'd already taken off, running in the direction of the crash, his arms pumping hard into the rhythm of his long strides, even before the final sickening thump of metal could be heard.

Abbey bit back a little sob of distress, her heart hammering, as she pelted along the tree-lined street to Nick's car. Hand shaking, she touched the remote locking button on the key-ring and whipped the boot open. She hauled his case out, slammed the boot shut and re-locked the car, turning to run back to the accident scene as fast as she could in her high heels.

Hearing the crunching sound of metal, two men had rushed from nearby houses to help.

'Right—let's do it, lads!' Nick took charge and, with muscles straining, they partially raised the heavy bike, bracing it against their legs.

'We need traffic lights or a roundabout there.' One of the men was breathing heavily with the effort.

His companion snorted. 'That won't slow 'em down. 'Struth,' he gasped and they strained again. 'One last heave should do it. You beauty...' he grunted as the motorbike was finally righted.

'Has someone called an ambulance?' Nick rapped, hunkering down beside the prostrate form of the injured rider.

'The wife will have done that.' One of the rescuers flipped his hand towards his house across the street. 'You got first-aid training or something, mate?' he tacked on, watching Nick's hands move with deft swiftness over the accident victim.

'Doctor.' Nick was curt.

'How bad is it?' Panting to a stop, Abbey dropped to Nick's side. She felt her throat dry. Dear God, the youth wasn't even wearing proper leathers.

'Severed femoral artery by the look of it.' Nick looked grim. 'See if you can find a tourniquet, please, Abbey. Step on it! We've got a major problem here.'

Abbey's hands moved like lightning through his medical supplies. In seconds she'd handed over the belt-like elastic band.

'How's his pulse?' Nick rapped, expertly securing the tourniquet around the youth's upper thigh.

'Rapid and thready. He's not responding to stimuli. I'll get an IV in.' Moments later, she was saying tensely, 'This is a nightmare, Nick—I can't find a vein.'

'Keep trying.'

'OK, I've got it.' Abbey's words came out in a rush of relief. 'IV's in and holding.'

Nick swore, his brow furrowing in concentration. 'BP's dropping like a stone. Come on!' he gritted to the youth's unconscious form.

'Don't shut down on me, sunshine—don't you dare!'

At last the ambulance siren could be heard. The vehicle screamed to a halt beside them, two officers swinging out.

Nick quickly introduced himself and Abbey, adding authoritatively, 'The patient's in shock. We need to run Haemaccel fast. And alert the hospital, please. We'll need a blood specimen and cross-match immediately on arrival.'

Within seconds the officer had passed the flask of blood product across to Nick.

'I found some ID in the kid's saddlebag, Doc.' One of the men who had helped lift the bike flipped open a wallet. 'Bryan Weaver.'

'Give it to the police when they get here,' Nick said grimly. 'It'll be up to them to get hold of the family. But at least we'll be able to give the hospital a name. Thanks, mate.'

'Think he'll make it?' the man asked soberly, as the youth was stretchered into the ambulance.

'Let's be positive.' Nick's response was terse.

'Are you coming with us, Doc?' The ambulance officer was hovering expectantly by the rear doors of the ambulance.

'Yes.' Nick slammed his medical case shut and hitched it up. 'Keys.' He put out a hand and touched Abbey's wrist.

'Oh—sorry.' She fumbled them out of the pocket of her linen blazer. 'He's lost a lot of blood, hasn't he?'

They stared at each other for a brief, painful moment.

Nick lifted a shoulder, the lines of strain etching deeper into his mouth. 'Let's pin our hopes on the Haemaccel keeping him stable until he gets some blood.'

'What about your car?' Abbey blinked uncertainly. 'It's locked but—'

'I'll get a cab back and collect it later.' He looked at her broodingly. 'And I haven't forgotten about Todd. I'll make my own way over to Sunningdale as soon as I can.'

'Yes—OK—thanks.' With an odd feeling of finality, Abbey watched as he swung into the waiting ambulance with all the grace of a superbly fit athlete.

'I'll be in touch,' he called to her before the doors closed and the ambulance was on its way, the chilling sound of the siren pitching into the quiet of the afternoon.

Abbey's thoughts were still scattered as she turned in through the wide gates at Sunningdale. Finding a vacant space in the staff car park, she took it thankfully.

Already she'd decided not to undertake the long drive back to Wingara. It would be quite late by the time she was ready to get on her way and she had no desire to travel the lonely highway on her own at night. Instead, she'd leave at first light tomorrow.

The rehabilitation centre was a pleasant structure with wide verandahs overlooking the well-tended gardens. There was much good work being done here, Abbey thought earnestly, but in Todd's case was it enough?

Her insides twisted. The force of Nick Tonnelli's argument had raised more questions than answers for her patient.

She was relieved to find the nurse manager, Lauren Huxley, still on duty in the Macquarie wing where Todd was a resident. In Abbey's opinion, the bright, vivacious, forty-something nursing sister had great empathy with the patients.

In the first few weeks after Todd's admission Lauren had kept Abbey in close touch with his state of mind, and now the two women had formed an easy friendship.

'We expected you much earlier,' Lauren said warmly, ushering Abbey into her office.

Briefly, Abbey explained about the biker's accident and her involvement.

'Tea, then,' Lauren said firmly. 'You do have time?' Her fine brow rose in query. She was well aware of Abbey's gruelling schedule on the occasions the young GP was able to get into Hopeton.

Abbey huffed a wry laugh. 'I've lost so much time today another few minutes won't matter. Tea would be lovely, thanks.'

'Good.' Lauren flicked on the electric kettle.

'You've had a face-lift in here since I was in last.' Abbey looked around interestedly, admiring the bright curtains and crisp paintwork. 'It's lovely, Lauren. So cheerful now and comfortable.'

'That was the idea.' Lauren placed the tea-tray on the table between them. 'The new committee's been pretty generous with funding.'

'So they gave you carte blanche?'

'Within reason. But I stuck out for the oval table and upholstered chairs instead of that huge monstrosity of a desk. It's so much less daunting for the families who have to be briefed. I mean, they're down in the pits already in lots of cases. Surely they don't need to be spoken to across a desk like less than bright schoolchildren?'

Abbey smiled, easing off her shoes and wriggling her toes in relief. 'Mmm, the tea's wonderful, Lauren, thanks.' They sat in companionable silence for a moment, until Abbey asked gently, 'How's Todd doing?'

Lauren chuckled. 'Actually, he's had rather a good day. I could even say a riotous day.' She paused for effect. 'He's learning to paint.'

Abbey looked stunned for a moment and then her face lit up with a wide smile. 'But that's wonderful! Who's teaching him? One of the OTs?'

'Mmm, Amanda Steele. She reckons our Todd has real potential.'

Abbey bit the inside of her cheek. 'This may not be the right time to tell you my news, then.'

'About Todd?'

'By a remarkable coincidence I was, uh, introduced to Nicholas Tonnelli today.'

'The *surgeon,* Tonnelli?' Lauren's eyebrows shot up into her long fringe.

'Sounds a bit incredible, doesn't it? I arrived at the TV studios this morning to take part in their usual *Countrywide* programme.'

'And?' Lauren leaned forward, her expression expectant.

Abbey gave a huff of uneasy laughter. 'When I arrived, the producer was hovering. Asked me if I'd mind a slightly different format. In short, what he called an impromptu debate.'

'What?' Lauren squawked. 'And he threw you in against Tonnelli? How did you fare, for heaven's sake?'

Abbey grimaced. 'Actually, I think I did better off camera. But I made sure he got the message on the state of rural health.' She coloured faintly. 'He asked me to lunch. And I found myself telling him about Todd...'

'I get the picture Abbey,' Lauren said with some perception. 'Is Dr Tonnelli suggesting a transfer to Dennison by any chance?'

'He suggested the possibility.' Abbey was cautious. 'And there seems no doubt he could get Todd admitted.' She hesitated, suddenly feeling her relative inexperience in this field of medicine. 'But if Todd's formed a special rapport with his new occupational therapist and is doing better, maybe it's not the right time to move him...'

Lauren shrugged philosophically. 'I think the decision is out of our hands, Abbey. We're all aware Todd is special but we can't go around with our collective noses out of joint if someone of the calibre of Tonnelli suggests he can be better rehabilitated elsewhere.'

'You all do amazingly dedicated work here, Lauren,' Abbey jumped in supportively. 'But I guess I have to agree with you.'

'I presume Dr Tonnelli will want to see the case notes and talk to us first, before he sees Todd?'

'Oh, yes,' Abbey hastened to clarify. 'He's already mentioned that's the way he likes to work. He wants to be as unobtrusive as possible.'

'Yeah, right.' Lauren snickered. 'Like a tiger going unnoticed amongst the deer.' She got to her feet. 'You'll find Todd on the verandah, I think. I'm off duty in two minutes. Oh—any idea when we can expect the dashing surgeon?'

'Not really.' Abbey explained about Nick's involvement with the biker. 'I have no idea of his movements while he's here in Hopeton. In fact, apart from a courtesy phone call to tell me what he proposes for Todd, I don't expect I'll be seeing him again.'

'I see…' Lauren's eyebrows lifted in mild conjecture. Surely that wasn't a blush on the face of the usually so cool Dr Abbey Jones, was it?

Back in her motel room at the end of the day, Abbey took a shower and then planned what she'd do with the rest of the evening.

Not much, she thought wryly, pulling on a pair of plain denims and a peasant top. Taking up her brush, she scraped her hair back into a casual knot, leaving several strands to feather out in the current fashion. Her motel was only half a block from the hospital so she'd walk over and hopefully find out the condition of the young biker, Bryan Weaver. After that, she'd pick up a take-away meal of some kind.

The hospital was well lit and Abbey drifted inside with a group of early-evening visitors and began making her way towards Reception.

'Hello again, Dr Jones.'

Abbey stopped as if she'd been struck. 'Nick…' Soft colour licked along her cheekbones and she did her best to ignore the swift jolt of pleasure at seeing him. 'What are you doing here?'

'I could ask you the same question.' Slipping a hand under her elbow, he gently drew her aside. 'I imagined you'd have been well on your way to Wingara by now.'

Abbey feigned lightness. 'Oh, it got too late so I decided to stay overnight. I'm really here just to enquire about our biker.'

'Snap.' Nick's eyes seemed to track over her features one by one before he went on. 'I've had a chat with the surgeon. The boy's stable and they're pretty hopeful there'll be no residual damage to his leg.'

'That's good news.' Abbey felt relief sweep through her. 'Did you happen to find out why he was travelling like that, so out of control? I mean there are wheelies and *wheelies*.'

Dark humour spilled into his eyes and pulled a corner of his mouth. 'As a matter of fact, I found his girlfriend waiting like a wilted flower outside Recovery. She told me they'd had a fight and our Bryan had stormed out minus his leathers. Young idiot. He could have killed himself.'

'Yes.' Abbey's look was sober for a moment, before she began to cast a restive look towards the entrance. 'Well, now I know he'll be OK, I won't bother the staff...'

'Have you eaten?' Nick asked sharply.

'Ah...no.' Abbey felt her throat dry. 'I thought I'd just grab a burger or something and take it back to my motel room.'

'That sounds like a crummy way to spend your evening.' His eyes narrowed on her face and suddenly the intensity of his regard hardened, as though he'd made up his mind about something. 'Why don't we link up, then? Have dinner together?'

In a quick protective movement, Abbey put her hand to her heart. 'I...wasn't counting on a late night.' She heard the slightly desperate note in her voice and winced. 'And you don't have to keep offering to feed me, Nick.'

His made a dismissive gesture with his hand. 'It's no big deal, Abbey. Do you have a

problem with two colleagues having a meal together?'

Oh, about a thousand, she thought, with the
kind of uncertainty she was feeling around
him. 'Put like that, I—guess it would be all
right, then.' She shrugged her capitulation.
'But I'm not dressed for anywhere grand.'

'No more am I.' He tipped her a lopsided
smile and Abbey blinked, taking in his appearance. He was wearing comfortable cargo
pants and a cream lightweight sweater, the
sleeves pushed back over his tanned forearms.

'I walked over,' Abbey explained, as they
made their way outside to the hospital car park.

'Makes things simple, then.' Nick slowed
his strides abruptly. Then, as if it was the most
natural thing in the world, he stretched out his
hand towards her. 'I'm round the corner in the
doctors' car park.'

Feeling somehow as though she was taking
a giant leap into the unknown, Abbey slipped
her hand into his.

They agreed on a small pub a few kilometres out of town, mainly because Nick said
they did a decent steak.

'I have an appointment first thing in the morning at Sunningdale,' he told her as they drove.

Well, he hadn't wasted any time. Abbey turned her head on the car's cushioned leather headrest and addressed his darkened profile. 'I had a chat with the nurse manager, Lauren Huxley, this afternoon. They'll be expecting you.'

He grunted a non-committal reply.

There were only a smattering of patrons at the pub.

'Mid-week,' Nick surmised gruffly, placing a guiding hand on her back as they descended the shallow steps into a sunken lounge-cum-restaurant.

'It's nice,' Abbey said perfunctorily, gazing around her at the exposed timber beams and the rich oaken sheen of the furniture.

Seated, they studied the wine list. 'They serve a nice local red here,' Nick said. 'Like to try it?'

'Fine.' Abbey managed a faint smile.

With their wine served and their steaks ordered, Nick leaned back in his chair, his green gaze travelling musingly over her face and dropping to the soft curve of her throat. 'Life plays strange tricks on us from time to time, doesn't it?'

Abbey swallowed. 'In what way?'

He seemed to think for a moment, before reaching out and taking her left hand. 'Well, when we woke this morning, we hadn't met.' Turning her hand palm up, he stroked the inside of her wrist with his thumb. 'We seemed to have packed quite a bit of getting to know each other in the past eight hours, wouldn't you agree?'

Abbey's heart rate had begun rocketing at the intimacy. 'I suppose,' she conceded, every nerve in her stomach tightening. She wanted to reclaim her hand without appearing like a frightened adolescent. Which was how she felt, she fretted, more than a little unnerved by the arousing effect his stroking was having on her senses.

She took in a fractured little breath, hoping frantically their steaks would arrive so that at least his hands would be occupied with his cutlery.

As if he'd sensed her unease, Nick released her hand abruptly, changing position to fold his arms across his chest. 'What time will you start back in the morning?' he asked, one dark eyebrow arched, the trace of a provocative smile touching his mouth.

'I'll be long gone before you even open your eyes.' Abbey touched the small medallion at her throat. 'I have to be back for surgery at ten.'

'Do you take any special precautions for the journey?'

'I make sure my vehicle is always in good running order. And I let the police sergeant at Wingara know when I'm about to leave. From that, barring mishaps, he's able to gauge my ETA. And why the sudden interest in my lifestyle?' she challenged, lifting her glass and taking a careful mouthful of the deliciously smooth merlot. 'I'm just a rural GP, Nick. I work my tail off with incredibly long hours.'

'Are you suggesting I don't?'

Oh, for heaven's sake! She didn't want to keep getting into these kinds of endless comparisons with him. She looked down at her fingers locked painfully tight around the base of her glass. She wasn't naïve. And she was not about to deny the wild kind of physical chemistry lurking between them—but other than that, they had nothing in common at all.

They each belonged in vastly different areas of medicine. Nick Tonnelli would be like a fish out of water in her world—just as she would in his.

CHAPTER THREE

THEIR steaks arrived, grilled to perfection and accompanied by a huge pile of mixed salad on the side. Abbey's mouth watered at the lushness of three kinds of lettuce, fresh tomatoes, chopped black olives and bits of avocado and red pepper thrown in for good measure. 'This is fantastic, Nick. How come you know all these places?'

His mouth tipped at the corner. 'Hopeton is my home town. I'm here for a few days R and R visiting my *nonna*.'

'Your grandmother?'

'I can see you're surprised.' He grinned and Abbey caught the pulse of deep laughter in his voice. 'Did you imagine I just leapt into life from somewhere? As a matter of fact, I have quite an extended family. Parents, two sisters, brothers-in-law, a niece and two nephews. They all live in Sydney now but my *nonna*,

Claudia—' he made it sound like *Cloudia* '—still lives here in the old family home. She's almost eighty-five,' he said proudly.

Abbey thought painfully of her own diminished family and asked quietly, 'Is she in good health?'

'For the most part.' His face softened into reflective lines. 'She's still feisty, demanding when I'm going to find a wife and continue the Tonnelli line.'

Abbey huffed a laugh. 'That's a bit archaic.'

'Hey, she's our matriarch! She's allowed to.'

'Have you ever been in love?' she asked suddenly, prompting raised eyebrows from the surgeon.

'I'm thirty-eight, Abbey. Of course I've been in love. Have you?'

The question hung in the air between them.

'I was engaged once.' Abbey's downcast lashes fanned darkly across her cheekbones. 'He was my trainer. Such an honest, generous man. But when it came down to it, I couldn't set a wedding date. And I realised I didn't feel about him the way I wanted to feel about the man I intended to marry.'

'And how is that?' Nick asked softly. Gaze lowered, he began to swirl the ruby-red wine in his glass.

Suddenly Abbey felt vulnerable. She blamed the wine and Nick Tonnelli's clever probing questions. She came back lightly with, 'Well, if I knew that, life would be a doddle, wouldn't it?'

They went quietly on with their meal.

Nick chewed thoughtfully on his mouthful of prime rump steak. He could hardly believe his luck in running into her again. OK, so maybe they had little in common except their medical training, but he knew enough about himself to realise he had to get to know Abbey Jones better. Though at the moment, how and where seemed insoluble questions.

But he hadn't got to where he was without overcoming a few stumbling blocks. He'd think of something. And it would all be worth it. He had a distinct gut feeling Abbey was as disturbed by his nearness as he was by hers.

His gaze lifted, straying momentarily to the enticingly sweet curve of her mouth...

'We'd better exchange phone numbers, hadn't we?' Nick kept his tone deliberately brisk. 'I imagine we'll need to consult about Todd over the next little while.'

'Oh— OK.'

Nick thought she sounded cautious and hastened to reassure her. 'You have my word I won't steamroller anyone, Abbey.' He placed his knife and fork neatly together on his plate and casually swiped his mouth with his serviette. 'I'll study Todd's case notes and take into account all you've told me before I make an assessment about whether the Dennison can benefit him.'

'But you're reasonably certain it can, aren't you?'

He shrugged a shoulder. 'I truly believe what they can teach Todd there will give him a new lease on life. Granted, not the kind of life he's been used to but, even as a differently abled person, there have to be possibilities for the sports-fit young man he once was.'

The thought of Todd's world being shaken on its axis all over again gnawed at Abbey. He was at such a vulnerable point in his young life. But at least she had Nick's promise that he would act with sensitivity. She could only hope Todd would speak up if felt he was being pressured.

'Time to go?' Nick had seen her quick reference to her watch.

'If you don't mind.' It was only when they walked outside into the foyer that Abbey realised his guiding hand at her back had shifted and now she was warmly pressed to his side. Her nerve ends pinched alarmingly. She didn't want this—an involvement with a big-time surgeon like Nick Tonnelli was crazy thinking. It could go nowhere, lead to nothing.

Yet she couldn't pull away.

'Oh—it's raining!' She held out a hand to the light sprinkle.

'Let's move it, then.' Nick grabbed her hand and they sprinted across the car park and threw themselves into the Jaguar. 'OK?' He arched a questioning eyebrow.

'Hardly damp.' Releasing the scrunchie holding back her ponytail, Abbey finger-combed her hair into a semblance of order and then bent to fasten her seat belt. 'How much longer will you be in Hopeton?'

'Only another day or so.' The engine came to life with an expensive purr and within a few moments he was nosing the car out through the exit and onto the road. 'Basically, I had a few days to call my own and I decided to spend them with Nonna. I like to keep an eye on her.'

Abbey could understand he would. He seemed to care a great deal about people in general. How much more would he care about his own family? His wife? If he had one—

'I have to be back in Sydney on Friday any-way to attend a charity do at the Opera House.'

Probably with one of those women he was always being photographed with on his arm. Abbey's fingers interlinked tightly and she wondered why the mental picture caused her so much anguish.

'It just occurs to me…' He sent her a brooding look. 'What do you do about a locum when you have to be out of the place?'

'Were you thinking of offering?' Abbey shot back with the faintest hint of derision. Run-of-the-mill rural medicine wouldn't interest him at all. He'd really consider himself slumming.

'Think I couldn't handle it?'

Abbey flicked him a puzzled glance, not sure where he was heading. She answered levelly, 'My predecessor, Wolf Ganzer, fills in for me. He retired in the district. And he keeps himself fit and in touch so it suits us both.'

Nick nodded and after a minute enquired softly, 'How about some music to carry us home?'

It seemed to Abbey that the journey back to her motel took very little time. One part of her was thankful, wanting it over. The other part, the silly, romantic part of her, wanted to prolong the evening, the contact with Nicholas Tonnelli.

When he nosed his car in behind her Range Rover in the parking bay outside her unit, she released her seat belt and looked at him. 'Thanks for this evening, Nick. And for agreeing to see Todd.'

'I don't want thanks, Abbey.' His eyes were broodingly intent and he lifted his hand to knuckle it across the soft curve of her cheek. 'But I wouldn't mind a coffee, if you have the makings?'

Abbey stiffened, the faint elusive scent of his aftershave catching her nostrils. She swallowed heavily. 'Um...it'll have to be instant out of those sachet things.'

'Instant's fine.' He sent her a slow, teasing grin. 'I love instant.'

'And my room's a mess.'

'Do I look like I care?'

Abbey could hardly breathe. This was the last thing she'd expected—or wanted, she told herself. She'd thought he'd just drop her off and—

'Come on, the rain's stopped.' Nick broke into her thoughts, releasing the locks. 'Got your key handy?'

She fished the tagged piece of metal out of the side pocket of her jeans and handed it to him.

'Nick…perhaps this isn't such a good idea,' she backtracked huskily. 'I mean, we should probably just say goodnight and…' She stopped and swallowed, his gravity making her frown. 'Why are you doing this?'

'I don't want the evening to end,' he said simply. 'Do you, Abbey?'

A beat of silence.

Abbey felt she was trying to walk through sand knee-deep. But she couldn't lie. 'No…'

Out of the car, she waited while he unlocked the door of her motel room. Nick ushered her inside and then followed her in.

Abbey had left the standard lamp burning and now its soft glow was drawing the small space into an intimate cosiness. She sent a disquieted glance at the double bed littered with her clothes, and pointedly crossed to the tiny kitchenette on the far side of the unit. 'Coffee won't be long.' Feeling as though her hands belonged to someone else, she filled the small electric jug, and set it to boil.

'I promise I won't keep you up, Abbey.' Nick fetched up one of the high-backed stools and parked himself.

She gave a weak smile. 'The coffee will probably do that anyway.'

'Do you have times when you can't sleep, however you try?' he asked, his voice low.

'Most people do, don't they?' Abbey tore open the sachets and shook the coffee grains into the two waiting cups. 'Especially people in our line of work. Sometimes, when I find it impossible to relax enough to coax sleep, I go outside and look at the stars.'

'I imagine they'd be something special out west.'

'With the sky so clear, absolutely. The stars appear like so many diamonds. Their sparkle is...well, I imagine it's like being in fairyland.' Vaguely embarrassed by her flowery speech, Abbey hastily made the coffee. She passed Nick's black brew across to him, watching as he sugared and stirred it.

'You make it sound wonderful.' His long fingers spanned his cup as he lifted it to his mouth. 'I'll come out and experience it for myself someday.'

Abbey refrained from comment. Instead, her shoulders lifted in a barely perceptible shrug. She poured milk into her own coffee and, beset by a strange unease, took the seat next to him at the counter.

'Don't believe me, do you, Abbey?'

She brought her head up, seeing the crease in his cheek as he smiled, the action activating the laughter lines around his eyes. And quickly lowered her gaze to blot out the all-male physical imprint.

But it took a while for her heart to stop beating so quickly.

Nick couldn't take his eyes off her. He felt his fingers flexing, his arms aching to draw her to him, to touch her hair, feel its silkiness glide through his fingers. The thought of something else far more urgent was enough to set his body on fire.

He raised his cup and took another mouthful of his coffee. Anything to stop the hollow, self-derisive laugh erupting from his throat, he thought ruefully. He cast about for a safer topic. 'Tell me about yourself, Abbey.'

'Oh. There's not much to tell— I'm fairly ordinary.'

'I don't believe that for a second,' he countered, hoping he'd managed to give the wry words the right touch of lightness. 'What about family? Siblings?'

She lifted one shoulder uncertainly. 'One brother, Steven. He's a GP, currently working at a health post in New Guinea.'

Nick's mouth compressed momentarily. 'So not much chance for weekend visits, then?'

'No.' Abbey shook her head. 'But we did manage to catch up last Christmas. I took a flight north and Steve flew south and we met in Darwin. It was good,' she tacked on, an odd little glitch in her voice. 'Really good. More so, because these days we only have each other…'

Nick was startled by the sudden change in her voice. She looked almost…haunted. 'Tell me,' he said quietly.

After a tense moment, she responded, 'Our parents were killed two years ago. One of those tragic road accidents. They were fulfilling their retirement dream of a motoring trip around Australia. They were somewhere west of Adelaide when a petrol tanker ran out of control in front of them and then exploded. They had no chance.'

Nick saw the heart-breaking emotion that froze her face for an instant and recalled how he'd rabbited on about his extended family. What a smug, self-satisfied clod he must have sounded.

He clenched his fists as if he wanted to pound at an unkind fate on her behalf. 'I'm so sorry, Abbey.' He shook his head. 'So sorry you had to go through that…' On an impulse he couldn't explain, he held out his hand, using the action to draw her up from her stool and into his arms.

There was a long moment when they were still. When anything was possible. Abbey took a shaken breath, tilting her face up to his, thinking she should stop this now. But the urge to touch him and to be touched in return was too great. Suddenly all her senses began to stir, unfold, waken. Her heart did a back flip in her chest. And she was waiting, expectant when Nick leaned forward to claim her mouth.

Nicholas. She said his name in her head, closing her eyes, revelling in the subtle warmth of his body as he held her closer. He made her feel wildly sensual, as if she wanted to go on tiptoe, take him to her, absorb the very essence of his maleness.

She made a little sound in her throat, waves of heat sweeping over her as she opened fully to the demanding pressure of his lips.

It was much too soon when Nick broke away from her. He turned his head a little, smudging kisses across her temple, her eyelids and into the soft curve of her throat, sending erotic visions to her mind, searing heat along each vein.

Abbey clung to him, clung and clung, her cheek hard against the warmth of his chest, while his arms cradled her as though she was infinitely precious.

She had no clear idea how long they stood there.

Finally Nick's chest rose and fell in a long sigh and he slowly untwined the hands she'd looped around his neck and pulled back from her. 'Abbey…this is a hard call but I have to go—while I still can.'

She lifted weighted eyelids to look at him, realising he was right. If he didn't leave now, there was only one way they could go from here and she wasn't about to let that happen. She shivered when his thumb touched her full lower lip.

'Don't forget me, will you?' His voice sounded raw.

She swallowed jerkily, wondering how her legs were still holding her up.

'I…don't know where any of this is leading, Abbey.' He sent her a strained look. 'But let's not shut the door on the possibilities…please.'

Then, as if he couldn't bear to leave her, he kissed her again. Just briefly but hard. 'I'm going...'

'Take care,' Abbey whispered, her eyes wide and dazed-looking.

'I'll see you.' He placed the softest kiss at the side of her mouth. 'Somehow.'

Abbey waited until she heard the throb of his car engine fade away before she trusted her legs to move. Was he saying he wanted a serious chance at some kind of relationship?

She lifted her shoulders in a shaken sigh, crossing to the bed. The idea was impractical. And totally impossible.

It took only a few minutes to pack her small suitcase for her return to Wingara in the morning.

Her head was spinning, and already there was a giant gnawing emptiness in the region of her heart.

On the other side of town, Nick sat sprawled on the old swing-seat on his grandmother's back porch, his lean fingers cradling a glass of neat bourbon. He felt dazed, as though he'd gone a round or two with a heavyweight boxer.

Hell's bells.

The ice cubes rattled as he rolled the whisky glass between the palms of his hands. Abbey Jones. A grunt of self-derision left his throat. 'Turned on like a randy adolescent, Tonnelli,' he muttered, downing the rest of his drink, feeling the spirit scorch his insides like a ridge of fire.

Impatiently, he put the glass aside and then shot out of the seat, leaving the swing rocking. Leaning against the railing, he lifted his hands, tunnelling them through his hair and linking them at the base of his neck.

His gaze narrowed on the old pear tree, his body attuned, hearing the stillness, and he faced the fact that emotionally he'd fallen headlong into the deepest water of his life.

But what to do about it?

Abbey's alarm work her at five a.m. Blinking her eyes wide open, she stared at the ceiling.

'Oh, no,' she groaned, as the events of last night enveloped her.

She felt the sudden heat in her cheeks, waiting to feel shocked at how she'd opened herself to Nick Tonnelli. But it didn't happen. Instead, she remembered the way he'd held her, the tenderness of his kisses before he'd left...

But how could they share any kind of future? she fretted, throwing herself out of bed and under the shower.

How?

Ten minutes later, dressed in the jeans she'd worn last night and a plain white shirt, Abbey swallowed a hastily made cup of tea. She'd get breakfast along the road somewhere, she decided. After she'd put some distance behind her.

Hitching up her bits and pieces, she left the motel quietly and only seconds later she'd reversed into the forecourt and nosed her four-wheel-drive out onto the road.

After almost an hour into her journey, Abbey suddenly realised she'd completely forgotten to call Geoff Rogers, Wingara's police sergeant. Well, there was a first time for everything, she thought dryly. Slamming the Range Rover into second gear to cut back on her speed, she pulled to a stop at the edge of the road.

Picking up her mobile phone, she activated the logged-in number, her gaze thoughtfully assessing the dun-gold grass of the paddocks on each side of the road. There was still something so untouched about Australia's wide open spaces, she thought philosophically. Something fearless.

It had had the hottest kind of sun blasting down on it for thousands of years, had seen drought, bushfires and floods but, despite all that, the country still came up smilingly defiant. It didn't surprise her that its stark beauty created a kind of spiritual awakening for many of the tourists who frequented the region…

'Wingara Police.' Geoff's voice came through loud and clear.

Abbey blinked a couple of times as though she'd been in a trance. 'Geoff, it's Abbey Jones. I'm just through Jareel township.'

'Abbey! You OK?'

'Fine. Sorry, I forgot to call earlier.'

Geoff chuckled. 'You're forgiven. Wild night out, was it?'

More like a wild night *in*. Abbey pursed her lips and scrubbed a pattern on the steering wheel with her thumb. 'I should be home by eight, Geoff.'

'OK, Doc. It'll be good to have you back. Ah...how's young Todd? Did you manage to see him?'

'Yes, I did.' Abbey hesitated. Literally everyone in Wingara was going to ask about Todd. 'There may be some better news about his progress in the not-too-distant future, Geoff. I can't say any more just now.'

'Understood. You always give us your best shot, Abbey. And it's not just me reckons that.'

Abbey closed off her mobile, Geoff's remarks warming her through and through.

It was a few minutes to eight when she coasted down a slight incline and glided into the township. But this time the familiar skip in her heart as the quaint wooden shopfronts with their old-fashioned awnings came into view was missing.

Why did she feel she'd left a part of herself back in Hopeton? The question buzzed around in her head and she bit off a huff of impatience at her crazy thinking.

Deciding she'd get herself sorted out before she went into the surgery, she took a side street to the rambling old house she called home. The place was far too big for her needs and she used only a tenth of its space, but it came with the job so the matter of where she lived had been largely taken out of her hands.

Almost absent-mindedly, she hauled her luggage out of the boot and made her way inside. For some reason, today the house seemed almost eerily quiet. How odd, she thought, catching the edge of her lip uncertainly. It had never seemed that way before.

A curious, unsettled feeling swamped her as she pulled stuff from her suitcase and piled her used clothing into the hamper in the laundry. 'For heaven's sake!' she muttered. You'd better get your mind back on your practice, Abbey, she told herself silently. Nick Tonnelli and his kisses are history!

But her body still tingled in memory.

Half an hour later, she'd freshened up and changed into a longish dark green skirt and pinstriped shirt. Stifling a sigh, she left the house quickly. Her surgery list was probably a kilometre long and she'd never felt less like work.

'You're back nice and early.' Meri Landsdowne, the practice manager-cum-everything greeted Abbey warmly. 'Good trip home?'

That word again. Abbey sent the other a wry smile. 'No dramas.' She took the few steps and joined Meri behind Reception. 'How have things been here?' Abbey pulled the desk diary towards her.

'Fairly quiet, actually. Wolf even managed to get his mid-week game of bowls in.' Meri made a small grimace. 'Frankly, I think everyone's been holding off until you were back. Ed Carmichael for starters.'

'Again!'

'First cab off the rank,' Meri commiserated. She gave a snip of laughter. 'Perhaps we could get a moat built around the surgery to keep him out.'

'He can probably swim like a fish,' Abbey surmised dryly. 'But he's a lonely man, Meri. He misses his days as a shearers' cook. We shouldn't be too hard on him.'

'Oh, Abbey, we both know half the time he only comes in for a yarn. And there are plenty of things he could be involved in. For heaven's sake, he's barely sixty!'

'I've had lengthy chats with him about what he could do to fill in his time.' Abbey flicked through the list of appointments. 'But nothing seemed to appeal to him. He reckons he's read every book in the library.'

'Oh, please!' Meri turned away to activate the answering-machine. 'Come on, let's have a cuppa before the hordes arrive. Did you get breakfast somewhere?'

Abbey gave a rueful grin. 'I meant to...'

'So, what distracted you, Doctor?' Meri sent her a laughing look as they made their way along the corridor to the kitchen. 'Or, should I say, who?' The practice manager cocked her auburn head at a questioning angle. 'You look...different, somehow.'

'New shirt,' Abbey dismissed, feeling her cheeks warm. Meri's green eyes were filled with curiosity.

A few minutes later, they were settled companionably over a pot of tea and the still-warm banana bread Meri had brought in. 'Heaven,' Abbey sighed, as she took a slice and bit into it with obvious enjoyment. 'Much nicer than anything I could've eaten at some greasy-spoon café along the highway.'

Meri raised an eyebrow. 'You never skip breakfast, Abbey. How come?'

Abbey felt goose-bumps break out all over her. 'Just preoccupied, I guess. Um...there may be some changes with Todd Jensen's rehab coming up,' she deflected quickly, and then stopped. There was no getting away from it. She'd have to fill Meri in to some degree about Nick Tonnelli's involvement. Meri was the first point of contact at the surgery and would need to be put in the picture when Nick began liaising about Todd. But her manager would be discreet. And in a small-town medical practice, that was always a great bonus.

'That's fantastic,' Meri responded softly, after she'd heard what Abbey had to say about the surgeon and the Dennison clinic. 'Audrey and Keith will need careful handling though,' she added thoughtfully, referring to Todd's rather fearful parents. 'They won't want him moved to Sydney.'

Abbey lifted a shoulder. 'That'll be up to Dr Tonnelli. And I don't imagine he'll have much trouble convincing them if he decides the Dennison is the place for Todd.'

'Charmer, is he?'

Abbey felt the flush creep up her throat. 'Not bad…' She hiccuped a laugh, her embarrassed gaze going to the floor. 'For a surgeon.'

CHAPTER FOUR

As Meri had indicated, Abbey's first patient for the day was Ed Carmichael.

'What can I do for you today, Ed?' Abbey looked up expectantly as her patient made himself comfortable, stretching out his legs and folding his arms across his chest. Abbey noticed that as usual he was dressed very neatly in a bush shirt and jeans and the inevitable riding boots.

'It's my right eye, Doc. Just noticed it getting dry and a bit uncomfortable, like.'

Abbey nodded. 'How long since you've had your eyes properly checked?'

'Earlier this year. I got new specs, bifocals this time.'

'No problems with them?'

Ed shook his head and then asked gruffly, 'Could it be a cataract?'

'That would have been picked up when you had your eyes examined. And cataracts don't just happen, Ed. You'd be noticing a clouding of your vision over many months or even years.'

'So I'm not likely to be going blind, then?'

'No, Ed. I think that's very unlikely.' Abbey blocked a smile, but really it wasn't a smiling matter. She sobered. Her patient's real problem was having so much time on his hands that he'd begun to imagine that every twinge signalled a medical crisis of some kind. She got to her feet. 'Pop over here to the couch now, and I'll have a look under some light. Just to make sure there's no infection that could be causing the dryness.'

Ed Carmichael obliged and, with as little fuss as possible, Abbey settled him under the examination light. 'Your eye looks fine,' she said, scanning the eyeball for anything untoward. 'Some dryness is fairly common as we age, though, but drops can help with that.

'Now, these will just help to make tears.' Back at her desk, Abbey scribbled the brand names of several appropriate eyedrops. 'Any one of these will be suitable and they don't contain an antibiotic so you can get them over the counter without a prescription. Use the drops several times a day if you need to.'

'And that'll help, will it, Doc?' Ed's pale blue eyes regarded her seriously. 'Not that I'm doubting you,' he added hastily, taking the folded piece of paper and shoving it into his shirt pocket.

Abbey smiled. 'It should. And as I said, this kind of thing is usually age-related. But as well as the drops, you could try holding a warm flannel briefly against your eye, say, three times a day. The gentle heat will give all those little nerves and blood vessels a wake-up call and a reminder to make some moisture.'

'Thanks, Doc.' Ed pulled himself up from the chair. 'I'll give it a go.'

Abbey worked conscientiously through her patient list, but felt somewhat relieved when Meri popped her head in to announce, 'Last one. Natalie Wilson, new patient with a bub.'

'Which one is the patient?' Abbey threw her pen down and stretched, rotating her head to ease the muscles at the back of her neck.

Meri placed the new file on the desk. 'Mrs Wilson didn't make that clear, actually. Just said she's recently moved to the district and wondered whether she could have a word with the doctor.'

'Better trot her along, then.' Abbey flashed a faintly weary smile at the practice manager.

'After that, I'll lock the door and put the kettle on,' Meri announced firmly.

'Come in, Natalie, and have a seat,' Abbey invited warmly, as the young mother stood uncertainly in the doorway.

'Thanks.' Natalie Wilson dipped her fair head and took the chair beside Abbey's desk. 'This is Chloe,' she said proudly, her arms tightening around the pink-clad chubby infant on her lap.

'She's gorgeous.' Abbey's look was soft. 'How old is she?'

'Four months.' Natalie swallowed unevenly. 'We're...um, new in town. Ryan, my husband, has just been appointed manager for the organic growers co-operative.'

Abbey nodded. 'So, how can I help you?'

'I— That is, we wanted some advice, really.' She hesitated. 'About immunisation for Chloe. Are there any natural alternatives?'

Abbey took her time answering. Whether or not to immunise their children was every parent's choice, of course. But in her paediatric rotation Abbey had seen the needless pain and suffering little ones had been put through as a result of not being properly immunised against what amounted to killer diseases.

'Natalie, I have to say, the short answer is no.' Abbey looked levelly at her patient. 'Is there a reason why you don't want your baby immunised?'

The young mother nibbled on her bottom lip. 'It's just you hear of such terrible things happening afterwards—like brain damage...'

'Those cases are extremely rare,' Abbey discounted. 'In fact, I've never seen one in all the years I've been practising medicine.'

A smile nipped Natalie's mouth. 'That can't have been so long. You don't look very old.'

'Sometimes I feel about a hundred.' Abbey gave a low, husky laugh, warming to the other's light humour. 'But there's no problem with Chloe, is there? She's in good health?'

'Oh, yes,' Natalie was quick to answer. 'And I'm breastfeeding her.'

Abbey's gaze grew wistful. The little one did seem utterly content. 'You know, Natalie, on the whole, most vaccines cause minimum side effects. And it's a sad fact that some of the crippling diseases that were around in our grandparents' time are making a comeback.'

'And that's because parents are not having their children immunised, isn't it?' Nevertheless, the young mother still looked doubtful.

'Look…' Abbey swung to her feet and went across to her filing cabinet. 'Why don't I give you some relevant stuff to read, the latest statistics and so on, and you and your husband can make up your minds? I certainly wouldn't want to pressure you. In the end the decision has to be yours. If you decide you want Chloe done, pop her back in and we'll take care of it, OK?'

'Thanks so much, Dr Jones.' Natalie took the printed matter and tucked it into her big shoulder-bag. She stood to her feet, carefully cradling her daughter in the crook of her arm. 'You've been really laid-back about all this.'

'You sound surprised.' Abbey held the door open for her.

Natalie's mouth turned down comically. 'I really thought I'd be in for a lecture,' she admitted wryly.

'No lectures here,' Abbey said with a smile. 'I can guarantee it.' She touched a finger to Chloe's plump little cheek. 'Take care, now.'

Abbey's afternoon surgery kept her busy with a trail of small emergencies, one of which was the situation of two lads from the high school who needed stitches after clashing heads during a game of rugby.

'How on earth can they call it a *game*?' Meri shook her head in bewilderment, watching the two walking wounded leave the surgery in the care of their teacher.

'Rugby depends on skill,' Abbey said knowledgeably, recalling her own brother's brilliance at the game when he'd been at university. 'The more skill you have, the better you can keep out of trouble on the field.'

Meri sniffed. 'I'm just glad I have daughters. At least they can't get into too much strife with their ballet.'

Abbey pulled across a couple of letters that were waiting for her signature. 'Except ballet dancers quite often suffer horrendous problems with their feet,' she pointed out evenly.

'Do they?' Meri looked appalled.

'Well, some of the professional ones appear to. It's all that stuff on points they have to do.'

Meri lifted a shoulder. 'Oh, well, Cassie and Georgia haven't advanced to that stage yet. And by then perhaps they'll be into something sensible like tennis,' she said hopefully.

Abbey chuckled. 'Or kick-boxing?'

'Don't!' Meri pretended to shudder and then smiled a bit grimly. 'When you have kids, there's such a minefield of decision-making involved, isn't there?'

Thinking of her earlier discussion with Natalie Wilson, Abbey could only silently agree. But as yet I don't have to concern myself with that kind of responsibility, she thought broodingly. And until the right man came along, the subject of having children was hardly up for discussion...

'Oh— Wolf phoned earlier.' Meri deftly creased the letters into neat folds and slipped them into the waiting envelopes. 'Did you want him to do a late ward round? If not, he's off gallivanting somewhere.'

'I'll give him a call and let him off the hook.' Abbey blocked a yawn, edging off the tall stool behind Reception and standing to her feet. She glanced at her watch. Almost five o'clock. 'It won't take me long to pop over to the hospital and do a round. Then, barring further emergencies, I'm off home.'

'You must be out on your feet after that long drive,' Meri commiserated. 'And you haven't stopped all day. Who'd be a rural GP, eh?' She turned aside to answer the ringing telephone. Several seconds later she was holding out the receiver towards Abbey. 'For you. It's Dr Tonnelli.'

Abbey felt her heart slam against her ribs. 'I'll take it in my room, thanks, Meri,' she instructed quickly. 'And you pop off home to the girls now. I'll lock up and set the alarm.'

'If you're sure?'

'Go.'

''Night, then.' Meri waggled her fingers, her look faintly curious as she watched Abbey almost skip towards her consulting room.

Abbey entered her office, her heart pounding sickeningly. Then, blowing out a long, calming breath, she reached out and picked up the cordless receiver.

'Nick, hello!'

Tonnelli curled a low laugh. 'Hello, yourself, Dr Jones. How are things?'

Personally—crazy, mixed up, scary. Take your pick. 'Fine. And with you?'

'Oh, can't complain.' A heavy beat of silence. 'I thought of you the moment I woke this morning, Abbey. Did you think of me?'

He'd spoken quietly, his voice so deep it made her shiver. Not only had she thought of him, she'd still had the smell of him on her clothes, the taste of him on her mouth. 'Nick...'

'I'm here.'

Another silence.

'Do you want me as much as I want you, Abbey?'

Her eyes closed. 'Nick—this is all a bit unreal.'

'What part of it? Our kisses seemed pretty real to me,' he said with a wicked chuckle.

'That's not what I meant.' Sounding strangled, she tried to block out the memory, the sweet shock when their mouths had met for the first time. When he'd leaned forward and teased her lips apart—and had kissed her as she had never been kissed in all of her thirty-one years.

'Not very experienced, are you, Abbey?' he asked gently.

Not with men of his calibre, certainly. With the phone still clamped to her ear, she swung up from her chair and went to the window, as if fighting against the sensual cocoon he'd begun weaving around her. 'Where are you?' she asked, desperate to normalise the conversation.

'Not where I want to be, that's for sure.'

Abbey's heart raced, thudded, missed a beat. 'Please, could we not talk about this?'

'We have to talk about this—*us*,' he went on doggedly. 'Surely it was more than just a momentary…*attraction*?'

'Perhaps it was,' she agreed tightly. 'But, Nick, we're hundreds of miles apart. Our *lives* are hundreds of miles apart!'

'So you're baling out without even giving us a shot? Turning your feelings off like a tap? You disappoint me, Abbey. I took you to be a far more gutsy lady than that.'

Abbey's fingers tightened on the phone. She wouldn't let him get to her. 'This kind of conversation is pointless, Nick, and if that's all you called for—'

'It isn't,' he emphasised almost roughly. 'I've seen Todd.'

Immediately, Abbey felt on safer ground. She swallowed. 'And?'

'I think the Dennison can help him. I've already begun liaising with Anna Charles and lined up an ambulance. Todd should be installed by next Monday. I'll have my secretary fax my findings to you.'

'Oh, Nick, that's brilliant.' Hardly aware of what she was doing, Abbey turned from the window and began to pace her room. 'And what about Todd's parents? It could be a bit sticky.'

'I've already spoken to them. They'll be in Sydney on Monday to help him settle in.'

So he had everyone eating out of his hand. Abbey felt the ground sliding out from under her. She gave a brittle laugh. 'When you decide to move, you really move, don't you?'

'There's no point in procrastinating, Abbey—about anything.'

Abbey's throat tightened. 'Don't go on as though we have some kind of future together, Nick. Tell me more about Todd's situation,' she sidetracked quickly. If she could keep him to medical matters, maybe she could cope—just. 'What about the fees?'

'It's sorted.' He sounded irritated. 'And to make Todd feel really at home, his OT is going to continue working with him.'

'Amanda? She's going to Sydney with him?' Abbey could hardly contain her disbelief. 'Just like that?'

'No, Abbey, not just like that.'

'What did you do,' she cut in harshly, 'bribe her?'

'Don't be extreme. At Anna's request, of course, I offered her an increase in salary. It's rather more expensive to live in Sydney than in Hopeton.'

It sounded like they were all closing ranks around her patient and leaving her out. Big-time specialists pulling professional strings, as though they were controlling puppets. 'Well, isn't that just typical?' she snapped, fighting against a sick kind of resentment.

'What?'

'Do you enjoy stripping expertise from rural health, Dr Tonnelli? Amanda Steele is one of the best occupational therapists Sunningdale has had in years. Her methods are nothing short of inspirational to the residents—'

'Abbey, you're putting the wrong spin on this.'

'The hell I am...' Abbey felt her throat close. 'I was right about you from the beginning, Nick. You just steamroller over everything to get your own way. Well, you've shot all your ducks now, so I hope you're happy!'

'Abbey, listen—'

'No, Nick, you listen. You said you were disappointed in *me*,' she went on, her words echoing with hurt and disillusionment. 'Well, I'm disappointed in you—more than I can say. I'll expect your fax!' She ended the call abruptly and promptly burst into tears. Her heart was shattering, destroyed just like the trust she'd foolishly built around him.

Nick felt as though his insides were tied in a thousand knots. And it wasn't a condition he was used to, he admitted uncomfortably. For the most part he had always been in control of his life. Now his thoughts were jumbled, too incoherent to organise rationally.

Thanks to Abbey Jones.

In an abrupt movement, he threw himself out of his armchair and prowled across the room to stare through the big picture window, his gaze reaching beyond the canopy of trees. Early evening mist hung across the mountains and already the sharpness of winter was in the air.

He stifled a sigh, turning and retracing his steps to the fireplace. Hunkering down, he carefully placed a new log on the fire and then eased the fireguard back into place.

'You have problems, Nikkolo?'

Claudia Tonnelli's snow-white head was lowered intently over her needlework but Nick knew his grandmother in her wisdom had missed nothing of his agitation. For an instant he was tempted to blurt everything out, as he'd done when he'd been much younger, and wait for her advice. Because she'd be bound to offer it, he thought dryly, uncurling to his feet.

'Nothing you need worry about, Nonna.'

'Come.' The elderly lady patted the space beside her on the sofa. 'Talk to me.'

Nick pushed his hands roughly through his hair. 'Not just now, Nonna. In fact, I think I'll go for a long run.'

During the days following her phone conversation with Nick, Abbey pushed all thoughts of him to the back of her mind. It was the only way she could cope.

His fax had arrived, together with a penned footnote from Nick himself telling her that Todd had been persuaded to let his wife visit and at least they'd begun to talk. Which is more than *we* are doing, Abbey thought bitterly, adding the faxed information to Todd's already thick file.

Nevertheless, every time the phone rang, she'd foolishly hope it would be Nick but, of course, it never was. Well, who could blame him? The pain in her heart welled up again, and again she beat it back. Why would he bother to call, when she'd told him off in no uncertain manner?

Had she been too hasty in judging his actions over Todd? Abbey shook her head. I just would have liked to have been consulted, she rationalised for the umpteenth time. Surely that hadn't been too much to ask?

Heavens, she'd have to stop this!

Resolutely, she made a notation on the file in front of her and placed it aside. Spinning off her chair, she moved to the window, absorbing the stillness, her gaze going to the distant low hills and then drawing back to the tangle of vivid bougainvillea that wound itself in glorious abandon across the roof of the pergola in the surgery's back garden.

'With such a beautiful view from my window, why on earth am I wishing I was somewhere else?' she whispered to the late afternoon air, almost absently glancing at her watch and realising it was Friday again.

And remembering it was two weeks and two days since Nick had kissed her. And held her as though he'd never wanted to let her go. She sighed, her thoughts becoming so bleak it seemed almost a relief to let the anguish engulf her momentarily.

Closing her eyes, she began to relive it all, losing herself in hopeless longing.

Reality came back with a snap when her door opened and was softly closed again.

Abbey spun round, coming to a shocked halt, her eyes snapping wide in disbelief. 'Nick…' His name came hoarsely from her throat.

'Your secretary said it was all right to come in.' He raised an eyebrow in query and waited.

Abbey's wits deserted her. She didn't know what to do. But all her instincts were screaming at her to bolt. To pretend he wasn't there. But that wouldn't work, he was blocking her exit. And not looking entirely friendly.

In fact he looked…*intense*, for want of a better word. Almost as if she'd never seen him before, she stared at the imposingly broad-shouldered physique, delineated by the close-fitting black ribbed jumper, his jaw jutting almost arrogantly over its poloneck. Blinking, she met the brunt of his gaze with its sea-green luminosity…

Her heart skittered. 'What—what are you doing here?'

'I've taken a month's leave.' He stood very still, the fingers of his left hand hooked into the collar of a leather jacket he'd slung over one shoulder. 'Do you think we can pick up where we left off, Abbey?'

Nick watched her eyes cloud and cursed himself for the ambiguity of his question. He allowed himself a small smile. 'Not from where you put the phone down on me, obviously,' he clarified.

Abbey winced at the memory, crossing her arms over her chest, her fingers kneading her upper arms. 'I don't believe any of this—that you've come all this way…' Breaking off, she stilled and gave a little frown. 'What am I going to do with you for a month?'

Green eyes regarded her levelly. 'Put me to work.' With a smile Abbey wasn't sure she trusted, he continued smoothly, 'You could do with some help, couldn't you?'

Well, of course she could. Abbey felt almost sick with vulnerability, and tried telling herself she wasn't feeling what she thought she was feeling, that her insides hadn't turned to mush, that his closeness wasn't making her nerves zing like the strings of a violin gone mad. She shook her head, asking throatily, 'Why, Nick?'

'You must know why, Abbey.' There was a slight edge to his voice and suddenly he seemed to come to a decision. Moving purposefully towards her desk, he unfurled the leather jacket from his shoulder and hooked it over the back of a chair.

As though he was staking some kind of claim. Abbey bristled. 'Being an MO here is light years away from your brand of high-tech medicine,' she pointed out, fighting to regain her poise.

'I'll adapt.'

Her heart skipped a beat. It could never work. Could it...? She looked at him warily.

'What, no comeback, Dr Jones?' Nick's mouth tightened fractionally. He moved a few paces to park himself on the edge of her desk and gazed at her broodingly. 'I scare the day-lights out of you, don't I?'

Snapping her chin up, she huffed forcefully, 'Of course not!'

His mouth folded in on a smile. 'Then that has to be a start.' In one easy movement, he straightened from his perch, taking the two steps necessary to gather her into his arms.

'Nick...' Her voice sounded breathy. 'You're taking a lot for granted.'

'Really, Abbey?' He brought her a few centimetres closer. 'Then let's make it worth-while...'

His lips ravished her, seduced her then teased her lightly, exquisitely until she shivered and arched against him.

She sighed against his mouth, her hands seeking out the solidness of him, her fingers digging into his shoulders, moving to shape the muscles at the base of his neck, going higher to run through the silky tufts of hair at his nape.

And then slowly he lifted his head.

Breathing hard, he tilted her face, one hand sliding among the strands of her hair. Scooping them up gently, he let them fall away in a cascade of gold and light. 'I could eat you, Abbey.'

Her insides heaved crazily. Locking her hands around his neck, she mustered a shaky smile. 'How would you explain that to my patients?'

His chuckle was warm, as rich as cream on apple pie. 'You're lovely,' he murmured deeply, his hand gliding to her breast and cupping it through her silk shirt.

'Nick...' She melted back into his arms.

And then abruptly pulled away.

'What is it?' A frown touched his forehead.

'Meri could walk in at any minute.' Quickly, Abbey finger-combed her hair into place. 'And speaking of Meri, if you're going to be working here, you'd better come out to Reception and meet her properly. And who knows? She'll probably find you the occasional chocolate biscuit if you bat that sexy smile at her now and again.'

'Really?' Grinning, he placed his hands on Abbey's shoulders, his thumbs stroking the soft hollow at the base of her throat. 'Do I have a sexy smile, then?'

'Stop fishing for compliments, Doctor.' She gave a strangled laugh, unfastening his hands and stepping back. After a moment she asked carefully, 'Was it difficult, getting time off?' She still felt amazed and slightly panicked at the lengths he'd gone to to be with her.

'The hospital needed a bit of persuasion,' he admitted. 'But they owed me the time anyway. They've appointed an excellent locum to cover my caseload, so in the end everyone's needs were met.'

Abbey felt riddled with guilt. 'I hope you won't be bored rigid here.'

'How could I be?' He sent her a dry look. 'I expect you to keep me very busy, Dr Jones.'

Abbey flushed. 'I...can't pay you much,' she deflected quickly. 'There is some extra funding to cover a locum but nothing like your normal salary.'

He shook his head. 'Abbey, the money isn't important. I wanted—*needed*—to spend this time with you. End of story. Now, where should I stay? I noticed several pubs on the way here.'

Abbey made a face. 'The Sapphire's the best but you don't need to shell out money to stay in a pub. I'm rattling around in a huge house that comes with the job. You can live with me.'

His mouth kicked up in a crooked smile. 'Live as in *live*?' he inquired softly.

Abbey felt the heat rising, warming her throat, flowering over her cheeks. She knew he was teasing her—well, she hoped he was. But she couldn't help wondering just what he expected from this month he was proposing to spend here.

And whether or not she was going to be able to meet those expectations.

'I meant to say, you can share my home— if that suits, of course...'

Nick's heart somersaulted. She looked even more lovely than he remembered and he suddenly knew without a shadow of a doubt he wanted to test the strength of this relationship as far as it would go. And despite the frustration ripping through him, he knew he'd have to tread very softly around Abbey Jones. Very softly indeed.

'Thanks.' He rubbed the back of his neck. 'That will suit me very well.'

CHAPTER FIVE

'I'LL give you the tour,' Abbey said, as they went out, closing the door on her consulting room. 'Then I'll take you home to my place and you can get settled in while I do a hospital round.'

'Why can't I come to the hospital with you?'

Well, no reason, Abbey supposed, nibbling at the corner of her bottom lip. 'It's all pretty basic medicine,' she warned.

Nick's eyes clouded slightly. 'Abbey, I'm on your patch now. I'm keen to learn about rural medicine.'

She opened the door of the second consulting room. 'I was just pointing out that there'll be none of the drama associated with Theatres.'

'I'm quite looking forward to the change of pace.' His voice was carefully neutral. 'But who knows?' He raised an eyebrow just slightly and grinned. 'You kind of lose the feel of general medicine when you detour into a speciality. I might turn out to be a real dud at your brand of medicine.'

As if! Abbey angled her gaze quickly away from the lively intelligence of those amazing eyes. 'This will be yours.' She led him into the reasonably sized surgery. 'Wolf uses it when he covers for me. Feel free to move things around if they don't suit.'

'I'll bear that in mind. But on first glance it seems fine.'

'Treatment room through here. It's quite large,' she said, pulling back a screen to reveal an identical set of equipment. 'Once upon a time there were several doctors working here.' Her mouth moved in a rueful little moue. 'But not for some years now.'

They moved on to the staff kitchen and walked onto the outdoor deck leading off it.

'Oh, boy,' Nick breathed in obvious approval, placing his hands on the timber railings. 'This is really something...' His gaze went towards the hills and the magic of a vividly pink and gold sunset. 'The last time I saw something like this was in Bali.'

'Have you travelled a lot?' Abbey came up to stand beside him.

'Some.' He lifted a shoulder. 'Dad took us over to Italy when we were youngsters and I've been back a couple of times. Done most of Europe. I worked in the States for a year, Canada for six months.'

She sent him a strained little smile, feeling like a real country bumpkin. Sadly, she realised she'd hardly travelled at all outside her own country. But there'd scarcely been time— or money, she reflected ruefully, considering the whopping great study loan she'd had to repay.

'Is your family very wealthy, Nick?'

A smile nipped his mouth. 'We never wanted for anything, I suppose. My grandparents established a vineyard outside Hopeton when they migrated from Italy. They never looked back. It just went from strength to strength.'

And brought in lots of money obviously. 'Is it still in your family?'

'Oh, yes. But they put in a manager some years ago, when we moved to Sydney. My parents run the sales and promotional side of things from there. Anything else you'd like to know?' he drawled with his slow smile.

'Sorry.' Embarrassed, Abbey looked away. 'I didn't mean to sound as though I was interrogating you.'

'You weren't,' he denied blandly. And then he frowned slightly, his eyes on her face with the intensity of a camera lens. 'Abbey, stop looking for the differences between us. This will work,' he said with conviction. 'We'll be good together.'

'Well, let's hope the patients think so,' Abbey waffled, feeling the warmth of his regard all over her. 'End of tour.' She turned abruptly from the railings. 'Let's put Meri in the picture and then we'll be on our way.'

'I'll follow you,' Nick said, as they left the surgery and made their way to their respective vehicles. 'How far is it to the hospital?'

'About five minutes.' Abbey waggled her bunch of keys until she found the one for the ignition. 'Seven if it's a foggy morning.'

Nick grinned. 'Perhaps I should invest in a pushbike? Save on petrol.'

'Or a sulky,' Abbey shot back impishly. 'That would go quite well with your new rural image. And there happens to be a beauty on display at the heritage village. Maybe they'd let you borrow that. I'm sure we could round up a nice fat pony to pull it.'

'And perhaps you could rustle up an old-fashioned Gladstone bag and a jar of leeches while you're at it?' Nick's eyes were full of laughter.

He'd never felt so light-hearted. And he was still wearing a smile as he tailed Abbey's Range Rover through the town proper and across the disused railway line. As she had predicted, they were at the hospital within a few minutes.

Nick got out of his car and looked around him. The hospital was a low-set building of weathered brick with several annexes at various points. There was a strip of lawn, faded to winter-brown, around the perimeter. And further over again, a windsock flapped gently in the breeze at the end of a large unfenced paddock.

'We do have the odd emergency,' Abbey explained, coming to stand beside him. 'The strip's regularly maintained for the CareFlight chopper to land.'

He shook his head. 'It's so quiet.'

'Mmm.' Abbey's gaze stretched to the shimmering water of a lagoon in a farmer's adjoining paddock and the wild ducks resembling tiny specks swimming serenely on its surface. 'It kind of folds in on you, especially at night.'

'You're not lonely?'

'For a while at first. Not now. But living here is vastly different from living in the city. In every way.'

'Yes.' Nick's reply was muted.

After a minute, they turned and began making their way across to the hospital entrance.

'Like me to fill you in about the staff?' Abbey flicked him a brief smile.

'Please.'

'We've a husband-and-wife team, Rhys and Diane Macklin, as joint nurse managers. They're terrific. Keep the place ticking over. Usually one of them is on duty. And we have a regular staff of RNs. They're rostered part-time as necessary. And there are two youngish aides, Zoe and Tristan. They're really just getting the feel of working within a hospital to see if they'd like to go ahead and train as registered nurses.'

Nick nodded. 'That sounds remarkably innovative.'

'Well, in a small place like Wingara, it can work quite well. And Rhys and Diane have the necessary accreditation to be their preceptors.'

'Who's the cook?' His grin was youthfully hopeful.

'I wondered when we'd get to that.' Abbey lifted her gaze briefly to the sky. 'Bella Sykes provides the meals at the hospital and also does for me.'

'Does?' Nick lifted an eyebrow.

Abbey chuckled. 'She looks after the doctor's residence which means she comes in a couple of times a week to clean and keep the place looking reasonable. She's an absolute gem.'

Nick looked thoughtful. 'The local community obviously values your presence enormously, Abbey. How will they respond to me being here, do you suppose?'

'Thinking of backing out, Doctor?'

Nick's jaw jutted. 'With you to hold my hand? No way.'

Diane Macklin was just coming out of her office as they approached the nurses' station. 'Abbey!' The nurse manager's dark head with its smooth bob tilted enquiringly. 'Three times in one day. Are you concerned about a patient?'

'With you in charge?' Abbey laughed. 'Not a chance. Um, Diane, this is Dr Nick Tonnelli.' Abbey turned to the man beside her. 'He'll be giving me a hand for the next few weeks.'

'Welcome aboard, Doctor.' Diane extended a hand across the counter. Her gaze skittered curiously from Nick to Abbey. 'I'll just bet you're old friends from medical school. Am I right?'

Nick tipped a sly wink at Abbey. 'I was a few years ahead of Abbey,' he deflected smoothly. 'Wasn't I?'

Abbey almost choked. 'Ah…yes.' Well, she supposed he would have been. He was several years older than her after all. 'And Nick's here for a holiday as well,' she added boldly.

'My first trip so far west,' he admitted, keeping the patter going but flicking Abbey a dry look.

'Oh, you'll love it,' Diane enthused. 'And I'm sure we'll keep you busy.'

Abbey stole a glance at her watch. 'Diane, we'd best get on. I'll just give Nick a quick tour of the hospital so he can find things.'

'Good idea. But do yell if you need anything, Dr Tonnelli.'

'It's Nick, Diane.'

The RN beamed. 'OK, then—Nick. Oh, Abbey, before you go…' Diane gave an apologetic half-smile. 'There was something. I wonder if you'd mind just having a word with young Brent.'

A frown touched Abbey's forehead. 'I've signed his release. He's going home tomorrow. What seems to be the problem?'

'Oh, nothing about his physical care,' Diane hastily reassured her. 'But he's seemed terribly quiet for most of the afternoon and he's asked me twice if I thought he was ready to go home.'

'That's odd.' Nick stroked his chin in conjecture. 'Most patients can't wait to get shut of us.' He raised a brow at Abbey. 'What was he admitted for?'

'Snakebite.'

'Oh—excuse me, folks.' Diane spun round as a patient's buzzer sounded. 'That's old Mrs Delaney.' She made a small face. 'Poor old love probably needs turning again.'

'You go, Diane.' Abbey made a shooing motion with her hand. 'I'll certainly pop in on

Brent. See if there's something needs sorting out.'

'Thanks.' Diane flapped a hand in farewell, looking smart and efficient in her navy trousers and crisp white shirt, as she hurried away to the ward.

'You know, he may just need to talk.' Nick backed himself against the counter and folded his arms. 'And, just for the record, I've never seen a case of snakebite.'

'That's not so surprising,' Abbey said, moving round beside him so that their arms were almost touching. 'Although these days, more and more snakes are being found in city environs and most of them are now being placed on the potentially lethal list.'

'Charming.' Nick's response was touched with dry humour. 'So, is it still the same treatment we were taught in med school? Compression, head for the nearest hospital and combat the poison with an antivenom?'

'Mmm.' A smile nipped Abbey's mouth. 'Much more civilised than in the old days. They used to pack the bite puncture with gunpowder and light the fuse.' Seeing the horror on Nick's face, she elaborated ghoulishly, 'You can imagine what it did to the affected part of the body.'

'You're kidding me!'

'Go look it up in the local history section at the library. It's all there. And there was another method—'

'Stop, please!' Nick raised his hands in mock surrender.

Abbey chuckled. 'Put you off your dinner, did I? Better get used to it, Doctor. You're in the bush now. Um, what did you mean about Brent?' She changed the tenor of the conversation quietly. 'That he might need to talk...'

'Just a thought. Give me the background.'

'Brent is sixteen,' Abbey began carefully. 'He's left school, works on the family property about seventy kilometres out. He was bitten on Monday last.'

'So he's been hospitalised all this week.'

'It seemed the best and safest option. To make sure there were no residual effects. And don't forget, if I'd released him too early, it would have been a round trip of a hundred and forty K's if his parents had needed to get him back in.'

'So you erred on the side of caution,' Nick said. 'I'd have done the same. Was it a severe bite?'

'It was a blue-bellied black snake.' Abbey identified the species with a shudder. 'And it got a really good go at Brent's calf muscle. Fortunately, he was near enough to the homestead to be found fairly quickly and he didn't panic.

'Out here kids are indoctrinated about what to do in case of snakebite. I remember when I'd been here only a few weeks, the principal of the school rang and asked when I'd be available to do "the snake talk".' She gave a low, throaty laugh, lifting her hands to make the quotation marks in the air.

Nick tore his gaze away from her smiling mouth. 'You said Brent didn't panic?'

'Ripped up his T-shirt, used it as a tourniquet and stayed put. He was visible from the track to the homestead and it was late afternoon. He knew his dad would be along within a reasonable time and he could hail him. It worked out that way and Tony and Karen brought their son straight in.'

'So, given all that, how calmly he appeared to handle things, is it just possible young Brent is now suffering from PTS?'

Abbey looked taken aback. 'Post-traumatic stress?'

Nick shrugged, palms out. 'It happens as a result of dogbites and shark attacks.'

Was it possible? Her hand closed around the small medallion at her throat.

'How's he been sleeping?'

'Not all that well, actually. But I put it down to the strangeness of being in hospital for the first time.' Abbey felt the nerves in her stomach tighten. Had she been less perceptive than she should have been where her young patient was concerned? She shook her head. 'He hasn't seemed to want to talk especially. In fact, I've been flat out getting two words out of him.'

'Well, there could be a reason for that.' Nick sent her a dry smile. 'He's sixteen, Abbey. His testosterone is probably working overtime and you're a beautiful lady doctor. The kid was probably struck dumb.'

Abbey felt the flush creep up her throat but then her chin rose. 'That's crazy!'

'Is it?'

'So I should try and talk to him, then?' Her hand clutched at her cloud of fair hair in agitation. 'Is that what you're saying?'

'Why don't you let me?'

'You?'

'I'm on staff now,' he reminded her. 'And your Brent may just open up to another male. This is how we'll handle it.'

Brent Davis was the only patient in the three-bed unit. Clad in sleep shorts and T-shirt, he was obviously bored, his gaze intermittently on the small television screen in front of him.

Abbey braced herself, going forward, her greeting low-key and cheerful. 'Hi, there, Brent. Just doing a final round.'

Colour stained the boy's face and he kept his gaze determinedly on the TV screen.

'This is Dr Tonnelli.' Abbey whipped the blood-pressure cuff around the youth's left arm and began to pump. 'He's from Sydney. Going to spend some time with us here in Wingara.'

'Hi, Brent.' Nick extended his hand. 'Dr Jones tells me you crash-tackled a death adder recently.'

Brent looked up sharply. 'Don't get adders this far west.' He sent Abbey an exasperated look. 'I told you it was a black snake.'

'So you did.' Abbey smiled, releasing the cuff.

'How did it actually happen, mate?' Casually, Nick parked himself on the youngster's bed and raised a quizzical dark brow.

Almost holding her breath, Abbey watched Brent's throat tighten with heartbreaking vulnerability, before he made faltering eye contact with the male doctor.

'I…was just walking through the grass. This time of year it's pretty long and it's dry, tufty kind of stuff. I must have disturbed the snake—maybe it was sleeping.'

'Don't they usually sleep on logs?' Head bent, Abbey was making notes on Brent's chart.

'Not always.'

'So, you disturbed it...' Nick folded his arms, and gave the boy an encouraging nod to continue.

'Bastard gave me one hell of a fright.' Brent made a sound somewhere between a snort and a laugh. 'It went straight into a strike pattern— like an S.' The boy flexed his hand and forearm to illustrate.

'Hell's teeth...' Nick grimaced. 'And then it struck and bit you?'

'Yeah. Quick as a flash.' Brent's demeanour had suddenly lightened with the enthusiasm of recounting his tale. 'I almost wet myself.'

'Hmm, lucky you didn't do that.' Nick's grin was slow. 'And Dr Jones tells me you kept your head and did all the right things until you were able to get here to the hospital. I don't know whether I'd have been so cool.'

Brent lifted a shoulder dismissively. 'Out here, you have to learn to take care of yourself from when you're a kid. Otherwise you're dead meat.'

Over their young patient's head, Nick exchanged a guarded smile with Abbey. This response was just what they'd hoped for. And, it seemed, once started, Brent couldn't stop. Aided by Nick's subtle prompting, he relaxed like a coiled spring unwinding as he continued to regale them with what had happened.

Finally, Nick flicked a glance at his watch. 'So, it's home tomorrow?'

'Yeah.' Brent's smile flashed briefly.

'What time are your parents coming, Brent?' Abbey clipped the medical chart back on to the end of the bed.

'About ten. Uh—thanks for looking after me.' He rushed the words out, his gaze catching Abbey's for the briefest second before he dipped his head shyly.

'You're welcome, Brent.' Abbey sent him a warm smile. 'And better wear long trousers out in the paddocks from now on, eh?'

'And watch where you put those big feet,' Nick joked, pulling himself unhurriedly upright. 'Stay cool, champ.' He touched a hand to the boy's fair head.

'No worries, Doc. See you.'

'You bet.' Nick raised a one-fingered salute.

Out in the corridor, he turned to Abbey. 'Told you we'd be a good team.'

Abbey's smile was a little strained. '*You* were good, Nick. Thanks.'

'Hey, you.' As they turned the corner, he tugged her to a halt. 'You look as though you've just hocked your best silver.'

She smiled weakly. 'I don't have any silver.'

'You know what I mean.'

Her mouth tightened momentarily. 'Why didn't I see Brent needed to unload all that stuff? He was relaxed as cooked spaghetti when we left.'

'And he'll probably sleep like a baby tonight. It's what's called getting a second opinion, Abbey, and I imagine they're a bit thin on the ground out here. Am I right?' he tacked on softly.

She nodded feeling the pressures of being a sole practitioner close in on her. 'But I would have sent him home still all screwed up—'

'Stop it!' Nick's command was razor sharp. 'You can't second-guess everything you do in medicine, Abbey. Imagine, as a surgeon, if I did that. I'd be residing at the funny farm by now. You do the best you can. None of us can do more than that.'

'But—'

He gave an irritated 'tsk'. 'Abbey, physically, your patient is well again. He's young and resilient. He'd have sorted himself out—probably talked to his parents about it, or a mate.'

'I suppose so…'

'I know so.' Nick's eyes glinted briefly. 'Now, come on, Dr Jones.' He took her arm again. 'You promised to show me through the rest of this place.'

Wingara hospital was old but beautifully maintained. Nick looked around with growing interest, deciding the wide corridors and carved wooden panelling over the doorways could have easily graced a fine old homestead. 'It's got a long history, obviously,' he remarked.

'Oh, yes.' Abbey nodded, regaining her equilibrium. 'Built in the days when Wingara was a thriving centre. In those days there was a permanent senior reg on staff and always a couple of residents, plus several GPs in private practice as well.'

'So, what happened?'

'The usual things.' Abbey's mouth turned down. 'The sapphire mine gave out, the rail line closed, the sawmill went into liquidation and people had to relocate to get work. Suddenly, it was the domino effect at its worst. Money leaves the town so shops lose business or fold. The pupil numbers at the school diminish so a teacher is lost, and so it goes on. But there's talk of the mine reopening and the local council has embraced tourism, so there's a bit of a revival happening.' She smiled. 'Things are looking up again.'

'What's the bed capacity?' They'd stopped and looked into one of the spacious private rooms.

'Only ten now. And, thank heavens, we've never had a full house since I've been here.'

'Do you have an OR?' Nick began striding ahead, his interest clearly raised.

'We have a *theatre*,' Abbey emphasised. 'You're not in the States now, you know.'

Nick laughed ruefully. 'Force of habit. Makes more sense to say OR when you think about it, though.'

Abbey looked unimpressed. 'Here we are.' She turned into an annexe and opened the door to the pristine operating theatre. Her mouth had a sad little droop. 'It's hardly used any more but Rhys insists the instruments are kept sterilised.'

Nick shook his head slowly. 'It's brilliant— for a rural hospital, that is...' His mouth compressed. He could comprehend more clearly now Abbey's underlying anger and frustration at the bureaucracy's continued neglect of rural medicine. Although he'd assumed things were improving...

He strode into the theatre then, as if to better acquaint himself with its layout, his movements sure and purposeful as he gauged the angle of a light here, stroked the tips of his fingers over a stainless-steel surface there.

'Do you want me to leave you here to play while I go home and start dinner?' Abbey queried dryly from the doorway.

Nick's head came up and he grinned a bit sheepishly. 'Be right with you.'

CHAPTER SIX

THE doctor's residence was next door to the hospital with a vacant block between. Again, like the hospital, it was of brick, a sprawling old building with a bay window at the front and with a large veranda on the eastern side, positioned to catch the morning sun in the winter and to offer shade during the hot summer afternoons.

As Abbey led the way inside, she had the strangest feeling a whole new chapter of her life was about to begin.

'Ah—sure there's enough room?'

Abbey wrinkled her nose at Nick's mocking look, her heels tapping as they walked along the polished hallway. 'There are four bedrooms, all quite large. You can take the one with the bay window, if you like. Bella keeps them all aired—don't ask me why.' She

129

opened the door on the freshness of a lemon-scented furniture polish. 'What do you think?'

There was something very homely and intimate about it, Nick thought. His gaze swept the room, taking in the fitted wardrobes, the dark oak dresser and bedside tables with their old-fashioned glass lamps. 'It looks very comfortable,' he said, his mouth drying as he looked across at the double bed with its plump navy blue duvet and lighter blue pillowcases.

He took a breath that expanded the whole of his diaphragm. 'Thank you, Abbey.'

Abbey's heart did a tumble turn. She swallowed. 'For what?'

'For inviting me to share your home.'

Suddenly the atmosphere changed, the light-hearted harmony disappearing, replaced with tension as tight as a trip wire.

Her startled eyes met his and widened, and her lips parted to take in a soft little breath.

It was too much for Nick. With a muted sound of need, he drew her into his arms. Raising his hands, he cupped her face, his thumbs following the contours of her cheekbones. She looked so beautiful, he thought, looking down at the little flecks like gold dust in her eyes.

Lowering his head, he tasted the fluttering pulse at her throat, before catching her lips, threading his fingers through her hair to lock her head more closely to his.

On a little moan of pleasure Abbey welcomed his deepening kiss, shivering at the intensity of her feelings the like of which she'd never experienced with any other man. Winding her arms around his waist, she urged him closer, closing the last remaining gap between them, tasting heaven.

But surely this shouldn't be happening.

With a tiny whimper, she dragged her mouth from his, her breathing shallow. 'Nick...' Her hand flew up to cover her mouth.

'Abbey?' He stared down into her wide, troubled eyes.

She held his gaze for a searing moment and then looked away, taking a step back as if to separate herself from the physical boundary of his arms.

In a show of mild desperation, Nick brought his hands up, locking them at the back of his neck. Did she expect him to apologise? Well, he was damned if he was going to. She'd kissed him back, hadn't she?

'I...think we need some ground rules.' Abbey wound her arms around her midriff to stop herself trembling. She licked her lips, tasting him all over again.

His jaw tightened. 'Are you trying to tell me you don't like me touching you?'

She flushed. 'That's not the point. This is a small community. We both have a professional standard to uphold.'

'You're having second thoughts about having me here?'

'No.' Abbey took a shallow breath. 'I'm just saying we need to be aware of how things look.'

A grim little smile twisted his mouth. 'In other words, to use the vernacular, you don't want it to appear as though I've come here merely to shack up with you.' And then he looked at her wary, troubled expression and his gut clenched. 'Look.' He pressed his palms against his eyes and pushed out a gust of breath. 'I'll get a room at the pub.'

'You don't have to do that!' Abbey shook her head and wondered why she was trying so hard to keep him under her roof. 'Just…as I said. We need to talk a few things through.' Seeing how his expression darkened at that, she added hurriedly, 'But we could do that later, perhaps—over a glass of wine or something…'

'Fine,' he agreed heavily. 'Is it OK if I take a few minutes to unpack? It's been a long day. I'd like to get squared away.'

'Of course,' she said quickly, almost breathlessly in her haste to try and normalise things between them. In a brief aside, she wondered if Nick was obsessively neat about the house. Oh, lord. She wasn't a particularly messy person but she did like to kick her shoes off the minute she walked in the door and she'd been known to leave empty coffee-mugs in odd places.

But I won't keep looking for the negatives between us.

She rallied, even dredging up a passable smile. 'I'll, um, grab a shower and see you in a bit, then. My bedroom has an *en suite* bathroom so feel free to use the main one.' She heard herself babbling and stopped. 'See you in a bit,' she repeated and hurriedly left the bedroom.

Barely forty-five minutes later, Nick joined Abbey in the kitchen, showered, his suitcase unpacked and his gear more or less sorted.

'That was quick.' She gave a stilted smile. 'I've just been checking the fridge. There's nothing very interesting for dinner and I wouldn't insult your ancestral palate by offering you a supermarket-brand lasagne.'

'I've eaten worse things.' His mouth folded in on a smile and he hooked out a chair to sit back to front on it, his arms folded along the top. 'Honestly, Abbey, I'm not pedantic about food. But I do like to choose what I eat, if that makes sense.'

It did. 'I usually do a shop on Saturday after I've finished surgery.' Abbey met his mild look neutrally, before her eyes darted away again. 'I guess we could make a list of the kinds of things we like...' She paused, as if waiting for his approval.

'Sure. That's fine with me.' He rolled back his shoulders and stretched.

Her expression lightened. Perhaps sharing living arrangements would work out after all. 'The Sapphire does a nice roast on a Friday,' she offered tentatively.

'The pub it is, then.' Nick kept his tone deliberately brisk. 'But I might make it an early night, if you don't mind.'

She suppressed a tight smile. 'And there I was imagining you'd want to hang about for the karaoke.'

'Maybe next Friday.' As if he was trying hard to regain his good humour, Nick's return smile was wry and crooked. Spinning off his chair, he placed it neatly back at the table. 'Let's go then, if you're quite ready.'

They took Abbey's four-wheel-drive. 'And while you're here, Nick, we split living expenses down the middle. OK?' They'd crossed the old railway line and were re-entering the town proper.

'Whatever you say, Abbey.'

She sent him a quick enquiring look. His remark had sounded as though he was humouring her. She frowned slightly. Suddenly the outcome of this month he proposed spending here with her seemed very blurred and uncertain.

'Be prepared to be well looked over,' she warned him. She'd parked neatly opposite the hotel and now they were making their way across the street to the beer garden.

'So, I shouldn't try holding your hand, then,' he interpreted dryly.

Abbey's heart thumped painfully. If he didn't lighten up, she'd jolly well send him home to eat that awful lasagne.

The beer garden was not overly crowded for a Friday evening and Abbey breathed a sigh of relief, scattering a smile here and there to several of the townsfolk who were obviously enjoying a meal out.

Seeing her action, a flash of humour lit Nick's eyes and he mimicked her greeting.

'Cheeky,' Abbey murmured, hiding a smile and taking the chair he held out for her.

'I always say, start as you mean to go on and at least now the locals will know I'm a friendly soul. I must say this all looks very civilised,' he sidetracked, looking around the precincts. And suddenly, he felt a lift in his spirits. Already he was sensing something special here in Abbey's world, not least the slower pace. His expression closed thoughtfully and he sat back in his chair, the better to take in his surroundings.

Fat candles on the wooden tables were giving out an atmosphere of light and shadow. And there was a sheen on the leaves of the outdoor plants dotting the perimeter of the raised timber platform, the fairy lights strung between them twinkling like so many diamonds. Or stars, he substituted, slightly embarrassed at his attempt at poetic language.

Tipping his head back, he looked up, his gaze widening in awe. The slender winter moon looked almost like an intruder amongst the canopy of stars, some of which looked close enough to touch, bright, like welcoming windows of light in a vast darkened abyss, while the myriad of others were scattered far and wide like so much fairy dust in the swept enormous heavens.

'Stunning.' Nick's voice was hushed.

Wordlessly, Abbey followed his gaze and felt her heart contract. 'Yes,' she agreed in a small voice, and didn't object when his fingers sought hers and tightened.

'You…haven't mentioned Todd.' The words slipped a bit disjointedly from Abbey. They were halfway through their roast dinners, their glasses of smooth merlot almost untouched beside their plates.

Nick gave her a brief, narrowed look and then dropped his gaze. 'I wasn't sure if the subject was taboo. But to answer the question you're probably burning to ask, he's going great guns. Even talking of getting involved in the sporting wheelies. In fact, I believe Ben Bristow, one of our champions from the Sydney paralympics, has been to see him.'

'Oh, that's fabulous. Sunningdale couldn't have managed anything like that for him,' Abbey said with quiet honesty. 'I imagine Todd would take to any kind of sporting challenge like a duck to water.'

'And Ben's influence will be invaluable.' Nick picked up his glass unhurriedly and took a mouthful of wine. 'His own story is not dissimilar to Todd's. Ben was a brilliant athlete, training for a triathlon event, when his spinal column was damaged after a road accident. It happened about five years ago. But he picked himself up, and now his list of sporting achievements would put an able-bodied athlete to shame. Consequently, he's become a bit of a hero, especially to disabled kids. He and Todd would seem to have that in common as well.'

Nick put his glass down and went quietly on with his meal, leaving Abbey feeling less than proud of how she'd berated him about his handling of Todd's care. 'I should apologise,' she said, and Nick arched an eyebrow.

'About how I reacted, when you told me what had been decided about Todd.' Her downcast lashes fanned darkly across her cheekbones. 'I—I know it's no excuse, but I felt, as his GP, I'd been left entirely out of the consultative process.'

His mouth compressed. 'I never in a million years would have wanted you to feel I'd put you down in some way. So that's why you let loose on me.' He smiled a bit crookedly, as if recalling the conversation. 'I must admit I was confused about your reaction.'

Abbey picked absently at her food. 'Perhaps I was feeling a bit...*intense* about things when you called.'

'Perhaps we both were,' he concurred quietly.

An awkward silence descended over them, until Nick rescued the situation smoothly. 'You know you were way off the track about Amanda Steele, Abbey. I didn't hijack her to the detriment of Sunningdale. Her moving to the Dennison was a reciprocal arrangement with one of the OTs there. And it's only a temporary arrangement until Todd gains enough confidence in his ability to cope.'

'Now I feel doubly foolish,' Abbey wailed. 'And on the phone, I must have sounded so...'

'Insecure?' Nick prompted with a smile.

'All right—insecure,' Abbey echoed in a small voice but nearly smiling.

'So...' He put his hand out towards her. 'Have we sorted that out now? Put an end to your...insecurities?'

She held her breath, looking straight into his eyes, feeling the sensual charge of his thumb tracing the top of her hand. Every nerve in her body was singing with sensation. Her heart thumped against her ribs and she wondered starkly whether, instead, her insecurities around this man were just beginning...

When she woke next morning, Abbey couldn't shake off the feeling of unreality.

But within seconds the soft closing of Nick's bedroom door and his muffled footsteps along the hall put paid to any fanciful idea that she may have dreamed his presence under her roof.

But where on earth was he going at this ungodly hour? She frowned at the clock-radio on her bedside table and stifled a groan. The man's mad, she decided, turning over and pulling the duvet up to her chin.

She was in the kitchen and dressed for work when she discovered the reason for him disappearing so early.

'Morning, Abbey.' He surged into the kitchen via the back door.

Her eyebrows lifted. 'You've been out running!'

Nick gave a warm, rich chuckle. 'Give the lady a prize for observation.' He'd obviously discarded his trainers in the adjoining laundry. He padded across the tiled floor in his thick sports socks. Looking thoroughly at home, he helped himself from the jug of orange juice Abbey had squeezed earlier and left on the counter. 'May I?' The glass was already half-way to his lips.

She nodded, suddenly utterly aware of the very essence of him. Heavens, he stripped well. She swallowed against the sudden dry-ness in her throat. He was wearing black shorts and a black and white striped football jersey that had obviously seen better days, but that only served to make him look deliciously rum-pled and as sexy as—

'Where did you go?' She held tightly on to her tea-mug, trying not to notice the ripple of his thigh muscles and the faint sheen of healthy male sweat in the shallow dip of his collar-bone where the neck of his jersey had fallen open.

'Someone's paddock, I think.' He drained his glass and refilled it halfway. 'I did a couple of laps of the helipad and then I climbed through the fence near the lagoon.'

'That would be the Dwyers' place.' Abbey slid off the tall stool and rinsed her mug at the sink.

He turned to her with a grin. 'They wouldn't have mistaken me for a wallaby and taken a shot at me, would they?'

Abbey made a click of exasperation. 'The farmers don't go round shooting randomly at anything that moves! Besides, you're way too tall for a wallaby,' she reproved, and he grinned, propping himself against the counter and crossing his ankles.

'Do you run every day?' she asked.

'When I can. And when I can't manage it, I use the air walker at home.' He raised his glass and swallowed the rest of his juice. 'I work long hours in Theatre. I need to be fitter than most.'

Abbey blinked. She'd never thought of it quite like that, but she guessed he was right. He certainly would need excellent physical stamina to stay alert and on top of his very demanding speciality. 'There's a sports track at the showgrounds,' she told him. 'I believe the early-morning joggers use that. I'll show you where it is later, if you like.'

'Thanks, but I think I'll stick to the paddocks. I like the sense of freedom running alone gives me.'

In a nervous gesture Abbey ran her hands down the sides of her tailored trousers. She couldn't help thinking Nick Tonnelli was one dangerous, potent mix and with no surgical list to keep him occupied for the next month, all that latent masculinity and coiled physical energy was going to need an outlet.

Just the thought that it all could be directed at her made her say, jerkily, 'Um, if you want breakfast, there's muesli in the pantry. And low-fat milk in the fridge.'

'I can't stand that stuff!' He shot her a rueful grin. 'Better add whole milk to the shopping list, hmm?'

Abbey gave him a pained look. 'I take it wholemeal bread is acceptable?'

'Very.'

'And canola spread? Or do you indulge in lashings of butter for your toast?'

He tapped her on the end of her nose with the tip of one finger. 'Canola's fine. Are you going across to the surgery now?'

'Shortly.'

'Like me to do a hospital round, then?'

Her mouth kicked up in a smile. 'Dressed like that? Hardly, Doctor. Even in Wingara, we like to observe some semblance of respectability for visiting medical officers.' With a quick twist of her slim body, she dodged the teatowel he threw at her.

Giving release to a wry chuckle, Nick turned to the sink to rinse his glass and then put the jug of juice in the fridge. 'I'll shower and make myself respectable first. That do?'

'Nicely. And when you've finished your hospital round, you may like to come over to the surgery. I'm sure Meri will be more than happy to clue you in about our style of paperwork and anything else you'll need to know about how the place runs. And don't forget I'll need your help with the grocery shopping this afternoon.'

'So bossy,' he grumbled, turning to refill the kettle at the sink, but Abbey could see the smile hovering around the corners of his mouth.

'I like to be organised,' she defended herself lightly, quite unable to stop her own smile. And five minutes later, as she made her way out to the carport, she was conscious of an absurd sense of light-heartedness.

Flipping open the door of her four-wheel-drive and settling in behind the wheel, she was suddenly overwhelmed with a rush of feeling. Oh, heck! Leaving aside the undoubted physical attraction Nick's body presented, was it just possible she was beginning to actually *like* the man?

Abbey's last consultation was over by eleven o'clock and Nick had joined her in the staff kitchen for a coffee-break.

'Do you normally finish about this time?' He took another slice of the apple cake he'd bought from the local bakery. 'This isn't half-bad.' He grinned, tucking in unabashedly.

'The way your eyes lit up when Meri mentioned chocolate biscuits and now this.' She pointed to the crumbly mess on his plate. 'I'm beginning to wonder if you've a shocking sweet tooth,' Abbey said laughingly.

'No worries, Doc.' Nick sprawled back in his chair, looking smug. 'This baby will run it off easily. Now, what about your Saturday surgery?'

Abbey became serious. 'I usually start at eight, earlier if it's necessary. Some of the rural workers have special needs, like a limited timeframe when they get into town. So I do my best to accommodate them. But normally I'm through by noon.' She twitched a wry smile. 'Meri books only what's essential, otherwise I'd never be out of the place.' She tilted her head in query. 'So, what about your morning, then? How was your ward round?'

'Different.' They exchanged smiles of understanding. 'Rhys was on duty so I made his acquaintance, and Brent's parents turned up early so I had a word with them as well.'

'And Brent seemed eager to go home?'

'Oh, yes.' Nick grinned. 'Quite an air of self-importance about him.'

'Mainly thanks to you,' Abbey said softly.

'Abbey, don't labour this. We're…' The rest of Nick's words were lost when Meri popped her head in the door.

'We have an emergency, folks.' She darted a quick worried look from one to the other. 'Rhys Macklin's on the line. They've had a call from a mobile at Jumbuck Ridge. One of a party of climbers is in strife.'

'I'll speak,' Abbey said briskly. 'Could you put the call through to my room, please, Meri?'

Nick shot her a sharp look, as they simultaneously sprang to their feet. 'How far is it to this place?'

'About twenty K's out.' Abbey pushed open the door of her consulting room, sensing his presence close behind. 'But we've no ambulance available today. We've only the one and it left this morning to transport a patient to Hopeton for kidney dialysis.'

'So we're it?'

'Looks like it.' Abbey picked up the phone.

Arms folded, Nick took up his stance against the window-ledge, listening with scarcely concealed impatience as Abbey fired questions into the mouthpiece. He could hardly comprehend the implications of having no ambulance available.

But surely to heaven they had an alternative procedure they followed in emergencies like this—or was it in the end all down to Abbey? He shook his head, the realisation of the terrifying uncertainties she probably faced on a regular basis shocking his equilibrium like the chill of an icy-cold shower on a winter's morning.

'Fine. Thanks, Rhys.' Abbey replaced the receiver and snapped her gaze to Nick. 'Right, we have a clearer picture now. Apparently, it's an abseiling group from the high school—seven students, one PE teacher, one parent.'

'And?' Instinctively, Nick had moved closer.

'The last one of the student team to descend pushed out too far. He came back in at an angle instead of front-on to the cliff and appears to have come up against some kind of projecting rock and knocked himself out.

Fortunately, his locking device has activated and that's saved him from further injury.'

Nick's breath hissed through his teeth. 'So, we can assume he's still unconscious.'

'Would seem so.'

'Then we'd better get cracking.'

'We'll take my vehicle.' Abbey began locking drawers and cabinets. 'And we'll need to stop off at home and change into tracksuits and some non-slip footwear and then swing by the hospital. Rhys will have a trauma kit ready for us.'

'I've been on to Geoff Rogers.' Meri was just putting the phone down as they sped through Reception. 'The police sergeant,' she elaborated for Nick's benefit. 'He'll do his best to round up an SES crew. But it's Saturday— the guys could be anywhere.' She bit her lip. 'Want me to stay here at the surgery in case…?' Meri drew to a halt and shrugged helplessly.

'Lock up and go home, Meri.' Abbey was firm. 'There's nothing further you can do here.

We'll co-ordinate everything through the hospital.'

Meri nodded. 'OK. Mind how you both go.'

'So, apart from the injured student, do we know what kind of scenario we're facing when we get to this Jumbuck Ridge?' Nick asked. They'd left the town proper behind and were now travelling as fast as Abbey dared on the strip of country road.

'The rest of the youngsters plus the parent have already made their descent and are at the base of the cliff. The teacher, Andrew Parrish, is at the top. But he's more or less helpless until help arrives.'

'In the form of you and me.' Nick scraped a hand around his jaw, considering their options.

'Yes.' Abbey's eyes clouded with faint uncertainty. 'Can you abseil?'

'I've done a bit. But not for a while,' he qualified. 'You can, I take it?'

'Steve urged me to get the gist of it when I'd signed the contract to come out here. I learned the basics at one of those artificial walls at the gym first and then Andrew kindly gave me a few practical lessons after I'd taken up residence.' She sent him a tight little smile. 'I didn't want to appear like a wimp and have to stand on the sidelines every time something like this happened.'

'As if abseiling would come under your job description,' Nick growled, his eyes on the brush of flowering red and yellow lantana that flanked the roadside. 'And how many times have you had to *throw* yourself into your work like this?' he asked pithily, clamping down on his fear-driven thoughts for her safety.

'A few, but it doesn't get any easier.' Abbey gunned the motor to take a steep incline. 'This is the first time we've been without an ambulance, though.'

'Then let's hope the State Emergency lads will get there before too long. I take it they'll make their way to the base of the cliff and wait for us?'

'Yes.' Abbey felt the nerves of her stomach screw down tight at the thought of the logistics involved in the retrieval of the injured youth, let alone without the back-up of an ambulance at the end of it. 'It's a pretty rough track but they have a kind of troop-carrier vehicle. And they'll be able to improvise so we'll end up with an ambulance of sorts.'

They were quiet then, each occupied with their own very different thoughts.

Physical education teacher Andrew Parrish was waiting for them at the clifftop. 'This is a real stuff-up,' he said grimly, after Abbey had skimmed over the introductions.

'So, do we have a name and how far down is the boy?' Nick demanded, already beginning some warm-up arm and shoulder stretches for the physical demands of the descent ahead.

'The lad's name is Grant Halligan,' Andrew said. 'Aged sixteen. By my estimation, he's about twenty metres down.' He looked at Nick as if sizing up his capabilities. 'Uh…I don't know how savvy you are with any of this, Doc…'

'I've abseiled enough to know what I'm doing.'

'OK, then.' Andrew looked at him keenly.
'Grant obviously needs medical attention so
one of you will have to drop down to him—'

'We'll both go,' Abbey cut in, her raised
chin warning Nick not to argue.

'I'll organise a harness for each of you,
then.' The teacher looked relieved to be getting
on with things. 'Doc, you're obviously physically stronger than Abbey so, as well as your
normal sit-harness, I'd like you to wear the
special retrieval harness.'

Nick's dark brows flexed in query.

'It's a full-body harness.' Andrew pointed
out the sturdy shoulder straps and leg loops.
'If Grant's out of it, and it looks as though he
is, you're going to have to attach his harness
to yours to get him down safely.'

Abbey bit her lip. 'That doesn't sound like
it's going to be terribly easy, Andrew.'

'We'll cope,' Nick snapped. 'Now, could
we move it, please?'

Silently and quickly, they climbed into the borrowed abseiling gear. Automatically tightening the waist belt above his hips, Nick felt the unmistakable dip in his stomach. Suddenly the smooth order of his operating room seemed light years away. And much, much safer.

'Now take these clip-gates,' Andrew instructed, handing Nick the metal locking devices. 'They're the best and easiest to operate in case you happen to have only one hand free. And when you've secured Grant to your harness, you can cut his line away.'

'With this?' Nick looked dubiously at the instrument Andrew pressed into his hand, no more than a small piece of sheathed metal.

'Don't worry. It's sharp enough to skin a rabbit,' Andrew said knowledgeably. 'So watch how you handle it.'

Nick grunted and slid the knife into an accessible pocket.

'Abbey, you set?' Andrew touched her shoulder.

'Yes.' She swallowed the dryness in her throat, checking the trauma kit's bulk which she'd anchored at the rear just below her bottom. 'If we're ready, then?' Her eyes met Nick's and clung.

'Ready.'

'Don't forget, now, Nick, you'll have Grant's extra weight on your line.' Andrew issued last-minute urgent instructions. 'So be aware of the sudden impact when you cut the line away. But I'll have you firmly anchored and it'll be fairly smooth sailing from where he's stuck right down to the base. Just steady as she goes, OK?'

'Fine.' Nick's teeth were clamped. Adrenalin was pumping out of him and already the tacky feel of sweat was annoyingly obvious down the ridge of his backbone.

Minute by minute his respect for Abbey's dedication to her responsibilities as a doctor in this isolated place had grown.

Along with his fears for her.

How the hell did she cope, living with this insidious kind of pressure? How? She was one gutsy lady—that went without saying. But surely enough was enough!

Whatever means he had to use and however he had to use them, he resolved he'd take her away from it all.

And sooner rather than later.

CHAPTER SEVEN

BOUNCING down the granite face of the cliff, Nick felt his skill returning. Cautiously, he cast a look downwards, just able to glimpse their patient in his bright yellow sweatshirt. 'We're nearly there,' he called to Abbey, who was slightly above him and to his left. 'Slacken off.'

'I hear you.' Abbey paid out her rope little by little, moving on down the rockface until she was alongside him.

'Right—this'll do us.' Nick signalled and together they swung in as closely as they could to the boy. 'And the gods are surely with us...' Nick's voice lightened as they landed on a ledge of rock and he began testing its viability. Finally, he managed to position his feet so that he was more or less evenly balanced. 'This should hold both of us, Abbey. Close up now.'

'I'm with you...' She edged in beside him.

Nick's gaze swung to her. She looked pale. A swell of protectiveness surged into his gut. 'You OK?'

'Piece of cake.' Her brittle laugh jagged eerily into the stillness.

Grant Halligan was hanging in space, quite still. But the top part of his inert body had drooped so far forward he was almost bent double into a U-shape.

Nick swore under his breath. 'Another couple of centimetres of gravity and he'd have turned completely upside down. OK, Abbey, let's reel him in.'

'Can you reach him from there?'

'Just about…'

With sickening dread, she watched as Nick edged perilously along the ledge, making the most of his long reach to grip the boy's waist harness and guide him in close to the cliff face. Lord, were they already too late?

Grant's colour was glassily blue. If they didn't act fast, he would be in danger of going into full cardiac arrest. And how they would begin to deal with that, suspended as they were on the side of a cliff, was something Abbey didn't want to contemplate.

Gingerly she positioned herself to receive Grant's torso and support his head. 'Right, I've got him!' Immediately she began to equalise the position of his head and neck, which would automatically clear his airway. 'How's his pulse?'

Nick's forehead creased in a frown. 'It's there but it's faint. And no breath sounds. Damn.' He dragged in a huge breath and in one swift movement bent to deliver five quick mouth-to-mouth breaths into their patient.

'Bingo…' Abbey let her own breath go in relief as the boy began to splutter and then cough.

'Best sound in the world.' Nick's voice roughened. 'But he's still well out of it. Grab me the torch, Abbey!' Automatically, he took Grant's weight so Abbey could access the trauma kit.

Tight-lipped, she leant into her sit-in harness and almost in slow motion slid her hand down, feeling around for the pocket containing the pencil torch. Convulsively, her fingers wrapped around it but then she fumbled getting it out, almost dropping it.

'Oh—help!' Her stomach heaved and she could feel the sudden perspiration patch wetly across her scalp under her safety hat. 'Here...' She swallowed jerkily and handed the torch to Nick.

Nick's face was set in concentration as he flicked the light into the boy's eyes. 'Equal and reacting,' he relayed, feeling the tightness in his temples ease fractionally. But they still had a mountain of uncharted territory to traverse before anyone could begin to relax.

So, no bleed into the brain, Abbey interpreted Nick's findings silently. She gnawed at her lip. 'His knee seems to be at an odd angle.'

'I had noticed.' Nick began feeling around for the clip-gates attached to a runner looped over his shoulder. The injured knee was an added complication. The sooner they got the kid down and treated, the better. He lowered his gaze to where Grant's injury was just visible below the coloured leg-band of his shorts.

The scraped skin was of little importance but his instincts were telling him that the puffy state of the student's knee and the blood seeping from the wound the rock had inflicted were matters for concern.

'He's obviously hit the rock with some force,' Nick surmised. 'Possibly after he banged his head and lost control. I can't do much from here. I'll look at him properly when we get him down.'

Watching Nick clench his fingers across the special clips that would anchor Grant to his harness, Abbey felt a swirl of nervous tension in her stomach. 'Are we about to try and hitch him to you now?'

'We can't hang about—sorry, joke,' he said heavily. 'But this could be tricky. I'm going to have to try to align Grant's body to mine, chest to chest. That's the only way I can anchor him to my harness.'

Abbey's nerves tightened. 'In practical terms, how do you want to work it, then?'

Nick gave an irritated snort. 'Like I do this for a living!'

In other words, your guess is as good as mine. Charming! She knew he was uptight but there was no need to snap her head off. Swallowing a sharp retort, she beat back a sudden wave of nausea, the result of inadvertently looking down.

'Abbey?' For a moment they looked at each other and Nick's mouth twisted with faint mockery. 'Sorry for my lapse just then.' His hand tightened on her shoulder, his gaze winging back to their patient. He took an obviously deep controlling breath. 'We'll manoeuvre Grant upright now. I'll help as much as I can, but I'll have to concentrate on getting him adjacent to my own body so I can secure the clip-gates to both our harnesses. OK, let's do it. But keep it slow and steady…'

It was useless. Abbey shook her head in despair. It was like trying to steady a ton-weight balloon with a piece of string. Grant was a well-built young man, his unconscious state only adding to their difficulties. And in their precarious position, it was well nigh impossible to co-ordinate the lift so the two harness belts were close enough to link.

'This isn't going to work.' Nick's lean, handsome face was stretched tautly. His shoulders slumped and he shook his head.

Abbey sensed his anguish. But they couldn't give up now. Grant's life could well depend on their teamwork. She pushed down her fears. 'Give me the clip-gates, Nick.'

His head went back as though she'd struck him. 'Are you mad? Grant's way too heavy and you're not wearing the right harness—'

'Stop trying to be a hero,' she snapped. 'And anyway, I didn't mean I'd try to take him. But we have to get a resolution here, Nick. It's not working—when you're steady, he's either too high or too low.'

'Well, I'd gathered that, Abbey,' he spat sarcastically.

She squeezed her eyes shut for a second and counted to ten. 'Could you link your hands under his behind and try to lift him to your waist? Then I could make a grab for his harness and snap you together.'

Nick's jaw tightened. 'Hell!' he spat the word between clenched teeth. 'I hate not being in control of this situation. I hate it!' But nevertheless he did what Abbey had suggested, gripping Grant, lifting him as high as he could, his muscles straining with the effort.

Abbey was pale and tight-lipped, knowing she had only the barest window of opportunity to hitch the two harnesses before Nick's hold on the boy would of necessity have to slacken. She steadied her breathing, conscious of almost choreographing her movements.

'I...can't hold him much longer.' Nick gasped, pulling his torso back so Abbey could use what little access there was between him and the injured youth. 'Now!' he yelled. 'Quick—or I've lost him!'

In a flash and remembering everything she'd been taught, Abbey used her feet in a technique called 'smearing', where most of the climber's weight was positioned over one foot to reduce the overall load on the arms. Twisting slightly, she turned her upper body so that her arm closest to the rockface could counter-balance her movement and give her other arm maximum extension…

'Now! Abbey…' What the hell was taking her so long? The muscles of Nick's throat and around his mouth were locked in a grimace and sweat pooled wetly in his lower back. His mind was so concentrated he hardly felt the nudge of Abbey's fingers as she secured one then quickly two more clip-gates to link the two men.

'Done…' Her voice was barely above a whisper.

Abbey hardly remembered how they'd got down. She only remembered the relief she'd felt when Nick had cut Grant's rope and they could begin their descent.

And there were plenty of hands to help them once they were safely on the ground. A subdued cheer had even gone up. Grant was released from his harness and placed on the stretcher provided by the State Emergency Service personnel.

Abbey divested herself of her own harness, dimly aware her legs felt as unsteady as a puppet's.

'I'll take that, Abbey.' Terry French, the leader of the SES team, hurried to her side to unclip the trauma kit and heft it across his shoulder. 'You did a great job.'

'Thanks, Terry, but I couldn't have made it without Dr Tonnelli.'

'He did well.'

Abbey gave in to a tight little smile. That, from the usually laconic SES leader, was high praise. She must remember to tell Nick—that's if they were still speaking...

'But it's the last time young Parrish pulls something like today's effort,' Terry said forcefully.

'Oh?' Abbey's eyes widened in query.

'He should've checked the ambulance was available, and when it wasn't he should've cancelled the abseiling. *And* he had no business taking that many kids without another trained adult. I'll have something to say at the next P and C meeting, I can tell you.'

Well, the Parents and Citizens committee could sort all that out later, Abbey thought wearily. All that mattered now was Grant's welfare.

Quickly, she pulled her thoughts together. She removed her safety hat, shook out her hair and began making her way across to where Nick was already leaning over the stretcher to attend to their patient.

Abbey could see Grant had begun to come round but he seemed confused and emotional. 'It's OK, Grant.' She bent to reassure him. 'You'll be fine,' she murmured over and over, rubbing warmth into his hands.

'Could we have the portable oxygen unit over here, please?' Nick began issuing orders, a deep cleft between his dark brows. 'And a space blanket.'

'Anything presenting yet?' Abbey watched as he palpated the boy's stomach.

'Feels soft enough so no spleen damage. Check his breath sounds, please, Abbey.'

'Bit raspy.' Abbey folded the stethoscope away. 'Could be a lower rib fracture. What about his knee?'

Nick was gently manipulating the swollen joint, his look intense. 'Fractured kneecap,' he said shortly. 'No doubt about it. But I can fix that.'

Abbey's gaze widened in alarm. 'You'll operate here at Wingara?'

'I thought that's what you wanted, Abbey.' His voice was suddenly hard. 'A specialist to come to the patient.'

Abbey bit her lips together. Nick's arbitrary decision had literally taken control right out of her hands.

Again.

Her mind flew ahead. Was their little operating theatre up to it at short notice? Given that it could be, this was still her practice and her patient. So, didn't that make her the MO in charge? But surely it would be petty in the extreme to start pulling rank when Nick's suggestion made perfect sense?

She had only a few seconds to decide on a course of action. Terry was already liaising with the CareFlight base. The sharp prongs of indecision tore at her and wouldn't let go.

'We'll run normal saline.' Nick was inserting the cannula in Grant's arm as he spoke. 'We don't want him shocking on us. And would you draw up twenty-five milligrams of pethidine, please? That'll hold him until we can get him to the OR.'

Abbey hesitated.

'What?' Nick's brow darkened ominously. 'Don't we have emergency drugs with us?'

Abbey took a thin breath. Grant's eyes had fluttered open again, dulled with pain, expressing all the heart-breaking youthful uncertainty of his situation.

'Abbey!'

She seemed to come back from somewhere.

'Do you need my instructions written on a whiteboard?' Nick shot the words at her with the lethal softness of bullets from a silenced gun.

Stung by his air of arrogance, Abbey jerked, 'Just who made *you* the boss here, Dr Tonnelli?' As soon as the words were out, she regretted them, for his expression darkened and his mouth tightened into a grim line.

She shook her head, biting the soft inside edge of her bottom lip. This was totally unprofessional behaviour. Why on earth did Nicholas Tonnelli bring out the worst in her?

And the best, another saner, kinder voice insisted.

Smothering her resentment, she drew up the required dose and shot the painkiller home.

'That's more like it.'

His growled patronising response infuriated Abbey all over again. She drew a deep breath, almost grateful for the diversion of Terry calling her name.

'Hey, Abbey!' Terry's tone was urgent. He jogged across, his face set in concern. 'The CareFlight chopper can't get here for a couple of hours. Three-car pile-up just south of Jareel. What do you want to do?'

Click! In an instant, Abbey knew the decision regarding Grant's surgery had been made for her. She took a steadying breath before she spoke, keeping her voiced instructions low. 'Cancel our request for a chopper, please,

Terry. Dr Tonnelli's a surgeon. He's offered to operate on Grant's knee here.'

The SES leader beamed. 'Well, that's a turn-up. I'll get onto CareFlight and let them know we don't need 'em this time.'

Meanwhile, *she'd* better get on to Wingara hospital. Her mouth drying with apprehension, Abbey pulled out her mobile phone. Co-ordinating everything was going to be the ultimate test of their staff's abilities to deal with an emergency. And she could only pray that Rhys would be co-operative and back the decision to open the theatre for Grant's procedure.

'It'll be fantastic to have the theatre in use again!' Rhys's enthusiastic response shot Abbey's doubts to pieces. 'What will Nick want to do?'

'He's going to be wiring Grant's patella. He can't be sure of the degree of complexity until he goes in, of course.'

'OK. I'd like to be involved and I'll do a ring-around for a couple of extra hands. Carmen and Renee should be available.

They'll be glad of the chance to hone their theatre skills, I'm sure,' Rhys said confidently.

Abbey brushed a fingertip between her brows, thinking quickly. 'We'll need to cross-match blood on arrival and X-ray as necessary. Especially, we'll need some pictures of his chest. There's evidence of a fractured lower rib. And could Diane come in and hold the fort while we're in Theatre?'

'Absolutely,' Rhys confirmed. 'No worries. What's your ETA, Abbey?'

Abbey ran through the logistics in her head, casting a quick look to where Nick was supervising the stretcher lift into the emergency vehicle. The improvised ambulance would have several kilometres of slow travel over rough terrain out to the road but then they should be able to pick up speed... 'Forty-five minutes maximum, Rhys.'

'Fine. That'll give me enough time to get prepped. See you in a bit, then.'

'Oh, Rhys.' Abbey spoke urgently. 'Andrew Parrish will have contacted Grant's parents.

They'll probably turn up at the hospital to wait for the chopper.'

'I'll have someone look out for them,' Rhys said calmly, 'and explain the change of plan. Tea and sympathy until either you or Nick can speak to them?'

'Thanks, Rhys.' Abbey felt a sliver of responsibility slide from her. 'That would be brilliant. See you soon.' Switching off her mobile, she moved swiftly to Nick's side.

'Ah, Abbey.' He inclined his head, his eyes gleaming with determination. 'We're about to go. I'll travel with Grant, if that's OK with you?'

'You mean you're actually asking me?' she acknowledged thinly.

His hand flew out, clamping her wrist, his dark brows snapping together. 'Don't turn territorial on me again, Abbey. This isn't the time.'

Abbey's heart thumped. Had she gone too far? 'I'll grab a lift back up to the top and collect my car,' she said throatily, feeling relief when his hand returned to his side.

'See you back at the hospital, then.' Nick's expression gentled. 'Uh…' He snapped his fingers. 'About anaesthetising Grant for the op—I forgot to ask. Can you help out? I can guide you if—'

'That won't be necessary,' she cut in. 'I did my elective in anaesthesiology at John Bosco's in Melbourne.'

'You wanted to specialise?'

Abbey stiffened. 'Is that so strange?' She turned away before he could answer.

Abbey could scarcely believe how smoothly the hospital was coping. She was still basking in a sense of real pride as she finished scrubbing.

The sound of the door swinging open sent her spinning away from the basin, and by the time Nick had begun scrubbing beside her, she was drying her hands and asking sharply, 'What size gloves do you need?'

He sent her an abrupt look from under his brows. 'Eight and a half, if the stocks can manage it. But I can get by with nine.'

'Rhys will have everything under control.' Abbey forced lightness into her tone. 'Even glove sizes, I imagine. Since the alert went out that you were going to operate, he's apparently been beavering away like you wouldn't believe.'

'I'm extremely grateful for his flexibility over this.' The tightening of Nick's mouth suggested her own compliance had been hardily won.

Abbey opened her mouth and closed it. This wasn't the time to start sniping at one another. They had a job to do on a vulnerable young patient and for that they needed calm and total professionalism.

Abruptly, she turned and left the little annexe and crossed to the theatre. Rhys had prepared the anaesthetic trolley perfectly and Abbey felt a rush of adrenalin she hadn't experienced for the longest time.

She'd do a brilliant job for Grant. And perhaps at the end of it, she might have actually appeased Nick as well. At the thought, warm colour swept up from her chest to her face, but there was no time now to consider why it mattered so much to have the wretched man's approval. But somehow it did.

An hour and a half later, the procedure was all done.

'Thanks, team. Fantastic effort.' Nick inserted the last suture in Grant's knee and signalled for Abbey to reverse the anaesthetic.

'Are this lad's climbing days over, do you think?' Rhys handed the surgeon the non-stick dressing to seal the site, and then waited with the bulky padding that would be placed over Grant's repaired kneecap.

'Not at all.' Deftly, Nick secured the wide crêpe bandage that would hold the padding in place. 'Does Wingara boast the services of a physiotherapist?'

Rhys nodded. 'Fran Rogers, the sergeant's wife, runs a practice from the sports centre.'

'She's good,' Carmen, one of the nurses assisting, chimed in. 'Sorted out the crick in my neck in a couple of sessions.'

'Sounds like we'll be in business, then.' Above his mask, Nick's eyes lit with good humour. 'OK, guys, that's it.' He stepped back from the operating table, working his shoulders briefly. 'I'd like Grant's leg elevated on pillows for the next twenty-four hours, please. And I'll write him up for some antibiotics and pain relief to be going on with.' His green gaze shifted from the nurses to Abbey. 'Would you mind finishing up in here? I don't want to keep Grant's parents waiting any longer than necessary for news.'

'I don't mind at all.' Abbey paused and then added huskily, 'That was a fine piece of work, Nick.'

Nick's eyes met hers and held. 'You made it easy, Dr Jones. We make a good team.' With that, he turned on his heel and left the theatre.

There seemed nothing more she could do at the hospital, so Abbey made her way home. Letting herself in, she acknowledged a feeling of vagueness, as if her body and mind were operating on autopilot.

It had been the oddest kind of day.

Walking into the kitchen, she looked around, registering her and Nick's breakfast dishes neatly stacked in the drainer.

A soft breath gusted from her mouth and she shook her head. Had it been only this morning they'd stood here fooling about like teenagers, exchanging light-hearted banter?

Absently, she turned on the tap and got herself a glass of water. Peering through the kitchen window as she drank it, she noticed that already the afternoon was rapidly drawing to a close, the sunset throwing huge splashes of dark pink and gold into the sky.

She lingered, watching several wood doves flutter in and out of the shrubbery before settling for the night. What was it about this time of the day that made her feel so introspective, so lonely, so strangely vulnerable?

'Mind sharing the view?'

Nick's soft footfall and equally softly spoken question had Abbey spinning round, a hand to her heart. She swallowed jerkily. 'I didn't realise you were home.'

'Have been for some time.'

His smile left a lingering warmth in his eyes and Abbey felt her heart lurch.

'I reassured Grant's parents and left a few post-op instructions with Diane. There didn't seem much else you needed me for. There wasn't, was there?'

She faltered, 'No—not really.' She desperately needed a hug but she couldn't tell him *that*. Her eyes flew over him. He'd obviously showered and changed into comfortable cargo pants and a navy long-sleeved sweatshirt.

Nick tilted his head, his eyes narrowing. 'You look shattered.'

'Thanks!' She lifted her chin, spinning back to the window, putting her glass down with a little thump in the sink. Was he saying she wasn't up to it? That she couldn't cope with one medical emergency? 'That's real music to my ears, I don't think!'

Nick clicked his tongue. 'Don't go all huffy on me, Abbey. I'm trying to help, dammit. Why don't you let me? For starters, are you hungry? I know I am.'

Abbey half turned to him. She supposed she was. They'd had nothing since his apple cake at morning tea. Perhaps it was hunger that was making her feel so hollowed out, so on edge around him. She nibbled the edge of her lower lip. 'We—we didn't get round to doing our grocery shopping, did we? And the supermarket will be closed by now.'

'I'm sure the pantry will yield up something edible.' His eyes captured hers. 'If not, I'll improvise.'

'You'll cook?'

'I don't just wield a knife in the OR, you know.' He flashed her a heart-thudding grin. 'I'll knock up some kind of pasta to delight your palate, OK?'

'Very OK.' Abbey felt her gastric juices react in expectation. 'There's bound to be a can of tomatoes in the pantry,' she said, warming to the idea. 'And I'm almost certain there's pasta of some description in a glass jar—'

'I'll find everything.' Nick's hands dropped to her shoulders to give her an insistent little nudge towards the door. 'Go and have a relaxing bath or whatever.'

Abbey made it to the doorway and turned back. 'There are a few herbs in pots at the bottom of the back steps—'

'Out, Dr Jones!' Nick waved an arm to get rid of her. 'I'm doing this. Go and have your bath.'

She sent him a wide-eyed innocent look. 'I prefer showers.'

He sighed audibly. 'Then have a nice relaxing shower, for Pete's sake. Now, scoot, before I lose all control and join you there.'

That did it. 'Consider me gone.'

Nick waited until he heard the soft click of her bedroom door, then lowered his head, bracing his arms against the bench. Hell, it was taking all his will-power not to follow her. But that was not the way. Every instinct was telling him that.

Ruefully, he looked down at his white-knuckled grip on the edge of the benchtop. It would be the death knell to his hopes if he rushed her. But holding back was hard— harder than anything he'd ever had to do.

CHAPTER EIGHT

ABBEY got out of the shower knowing she was in a state of wild anticipation of the evening ahead.

Oh, for heaven's sake, get a grip! Giving herself the silent admonishment, she padded through to the bedroom. It was merely going to be a quiet evening at home with a colleague, accompanied by an impromptu meal. And perhaps said colleague was a dud cook anyway and the food would be awful...

Who was she kidding? She gave a jagged laugh, throwing her softest, sleekest pair of jeans across the bed, then collected lacy underclothes from the bureau drawer.

The evening wasn't about colleagues or food, good or bad. It was about a man and a woman. And they both knew it!

With an effort, she managed to get her thoughts under control, dressing quickly in her

184

jeans and a close-fitting red V-necked pullover. The colour gave her a sense of power, she decided. Besides, it went well with her complexion.

She took in a calming breath and then picked up her brush, stroking it almost roughly through her hair. In a final dash of bravado, she coloured her mouth expertly with a rose lipstick and fluffed on a light spray of perfume. After one last glimpse in the mirror, she left her bedroom and made her way along the hallway to the kitchen.

Nick was bent over the cook top. The pasta was boiling merrily and he was stirring something in a saucepan on another hotplate. 'Something smells good,' she said, sniffing the appetising aroma as she peered over his shoulder.

'It's getting there.' Grinning, he turned his head and kissed her, a sweet undemanding little smooch that took her by surprise. 'What about setting the table?'

'So, does this concoction have a name?' Abbey got down some large bowls for their pasta.

Nick gave the pot a final stir. 'Officially, Tortiglioni alla zingara. But this version has sweet potato instead of aubergine, otherwise it's pretty much authentic.' He drained the pasta with a flourish and gave it a shake. 'I've left the Parmesan separate—not everyone cares for it.'

Her mouth watering, Abbey watched as he swirled the pasta into a large bowl and then folded the rich red sauce through it. 'It's hardly Italian fare without it, though, is it?'

'Probably not.' Lifting a hand, he playfully ran the tip of his finger down her nose and across the top of her cheek. 'I found some oregano as well in one of your pots. I haven't managed to prepare it yet.'

'I'll do that.' Her heart gave a sideways skip and she gave an off-key little laugh, stepping away from him to the worktop. She took up the rather scraggy-looking bunch of leaves. 'Should I chop it or tear it?'

'Roughly chop, please.' Nick was precise. 'And then chuck it over the pasta.'

They ate with obvious enjoyment. 'How did I do, then?' Nick gave her a look so warm that Abbey caught her breath.

She coloured faintly. 'You did so well I might just keep you.' She laughed. 'Honestly, Nick, this is wonderful.'

He lifted a shoulder modestly. 'But, then, we were both starving, weren't we? Probably bread and cheese would've seemed like a feast.' Something flickered in his gaze, something Abbey couldn't immediately define, and then he looked away.

'It's still very early, isn't it?' They'd come to the end of the meal and Abbey cast around for something to say, and in the process sent a distracted look at the quaint little cuckoo clock on the wall.

'Meaning what, exactly?' Nick's gaze shimmered over her face and then roamed to register the gleam of lamplight in her hair and on the ridge of her collar-bone. Hell's bells, he could almost taste her...

Abbey felt panic-stricken. What on earth were they to do with the long evening ahead?

What did Nick expect to do? Her teeth caught on her lower lip as she drummed up an awkward smile. 'Meaning, do you play Scrabble—or Trivial Pursuit?'

His gaze went briefly to the ceiling. 'I've a much better idea. Let's make some coffee and take it through to the lounge. Is it cool enough for a fire, do you suppose?'

'Oh, yes, I should think so.' Glad of something to do, Abbey shot to her feet. 'The kindling's all there. If you'd do that, I'll make the coffee.'

She took as long as she dared. Finally, when it was obvious she couldn't delay any longer, she picked up the tray of coffee and walked through the arched doorway to the lounge room.

Nick had the fire going and he'd lit one table lamp at the end of the comfortable old sofa. He was sitting under the light, leafing through one of her *Town and Country* magazines, and when she walked in he looked directly at her, his face still in shadow. 'I thought you must have gone to Brazil for the coffee beans,' he said blandly.

Abbey felt herself beginning to flush. 'Sorry if I was a bit long. I stacked the dishwasher as well.'

He raised a dark eyebrow. 'I didn't know we had one.'

'It's in the laundry for the moment.' She placed the tray on the mahogany chest in front of the fire. 'We're still waiting for the plumber to do the necessary adjustment so it can go in the kitchen,' she lamented. 'It certainly would make things a lot easier.'

'Well, don't look at me!' Nick raised his hands in mock horror. 'My mechanical skills stop a long way short of anything to do with plumbing.'

'Surely you can replace a tap washer?' she teased.

He looked baffled. 'Taps have washers? That's news to me.'

Abbey's mouth tucked in on a grin as she sent down the plunger on the coffee. They were shadow dancing again—fooling about, as if it was obvious to both of them that if their conversation became too serious, too personal, it would all be too confronting.

And because anything else would have seemed ridiculous, she took her place beside him on the sofa, feeling his gaze on her as she leant over and poured his coffee.

'Thanks.' Nick's fingers brushed hers as she handed him the steaming brew. 'That smells wonderful.' His mouth quirked in the faintest smile. 'Well worth the trip to Brazil.'

Abbey hiccuped a laugh and their gazes met and clung. His look was warm and heavy and on reflex she moistened parched lips. His gaze dropped to her mouth, almost burning her with intent.

With fingers that shook, Abbey poured her own coffee, taking several deep breaths to steady herself.

'How long does your contract have to run?' he asked.

She swallowed the sudden dryness in her throat. Where on earth had that sprung from? 'Six months or thereabouts. Why?'

'Just wondered.' He took a careful mouthful of his coffee. 'Any plans to come back to the coast?'

At his question, their gazes swivelled and caught and Nick's eyes held hers for a long moment, before he looked down broodingly into his coffee-cup.

'I…hadn't actually thought about it.' Leaving her coffee untouched on the tray, Abbey wrapped her arms around her midriff, as if warding off his question. 'It would be very difficult to find a replacement. The people had been waiting for over a year for a full-time medical officer when I came.'

'So, what are you saying?' Nick's jaw hardened. 'That you're bound here by some kind of emotional and ethical blackmail?'

Abbey's sound of disgust indicated what she thought of that. 'Does it occur to you I might like it here?'

'It sure looked like you were having a barrel of laughs coming down that cliff today,' he growled. 'I hate the thought of you taking those kinds of risks, Abbey.'

She bristled. 'For heaven's sake, Nick! It's not like Wingara has a team of paramedics on call. Attending the scene of an accident is my job!'

The silence fell thickly between them.

Jerkily, Abbey picked up her coffee, taking several quick mouthfuls. 'You can't tell me what to do, Nick,' she said quietly. 'It's none of your business anyway.'

'What if I were to make it my business?'

'And how would you do that?' More composed now, although her heart was rattling against her ribcage, she turned her head towards him, leaning back into the softness of the sofa, her coffee balanced high against her chest.

'Convince you to come back to Sydney with me.' His eyes locked with hers, dark in shadow, caressing, powerful.

'You're asking me to dump my patients?' She barely controlled the accusation in her voice. 'I'd have to find your offer pretty damned irresistible to make me even consider that.' Their eyes skittered away from each other and then reconnected and all of a sudden, once again, it was dangerous territory.

'Perhaps you will.'

Abbey opened her mouth and closed it and then opened it again. 'So, the chase is on, then?' she blurted, almost unable to believe they were having this conversation.

He sent her a dry smile. 'If you want to put it like that, yes, Abbey Jones, the chase is on.'

His meaning was quite clear and her response was instinctive. 'This is insane, Nick. But much more fun than Scrabble, I have to say.' She finished her coffee slowly and placed her cup back on the tray. 'So, what would you like to do now?' She tilted a slightly challenging look at him, letting her shoes drop to the floor and curling her legs beneath her.

Nick's sudden action made her jump.

'What are you doing?' she gasped, as he swung her feet around and then lifted them onto his lap.

'Just this…' With strong, supple hands, he began to massage the soles of her feet.

Abbey felt like purring. No one had ever massaged her feet before. She'd had no idea anything could be so seductive and, in a way, so liberating... 'I shouldn't be letting you do this.'

'Indulge me, hmm?' His dark head came up, his mouth curling slightly, as his hands moved up and down her feet and ankles, first her left and then right. 'Good?'

Abbey took a shaken breath then smiled, false brightness covering a multitude of mixed emotions. 'It's fantastic.'

As he'd known it would be.

'I could go to sleep,' she murmured a bit later. Her head had dropped back on the cushions and her whole body felt like liquid silk.

'I'll help you to bed,' Nick promised softly.

'No, you won't.' His words had her shooting determinedly upright, bracing her hand against the back of the sofa and preparing to lever herself off.

But Nick was quicker. Before she could properly make her move, his arms had cradled her and scooped her up. 'Bed for you, Dr

Jones,' he murmured into her hair. 'It's been a very long, very full day.'

'It's not that late.'

'Maybe it's later than you think.'

'Nick, put me down!' But her outrage was muted and only half-hearted.

'Don't argue, Abbey.' He carried her easily as if she weighed no more than an armful of roses.

She made a tiny sound in her throat. It felt so good in his arms... So safe. Safe? Now, that was odd... She was aware of him opening the door to her bedroom and carrying her inside.

The moon was out in earnest now, striping the walls and the white bed cover with soft light.

'Nick...?' Abbey reached up to stroke his face, and felt him stiffen. 'Will you start the dishwasher?'

His mouth twitched. 'You're a real romantic.'

'You're trying to seduce me...'

'Of course I am.' She felt his smile on her temple as he pressed a kiss there. 'But not tonight.' He lowered her to the bed. 'Sleep well.'

'Mmm.' Her eyes were already closed.

Abbey rose earlier than usual next morning but it was obvious Nick had risen earlier still. She found him in the kitchen, his hands wrapped round a mug of tea.

'Oh…' Her gaze ran over his attire. 'You've already done your run.' Her tone showed her disappointment. She'd been hoping some exercise would have helped chase away the inner turmoil she'd felt from the moment she'd woken. 'I was going to come with you.'

'You have to be up early to catch me.' The sides of his mouth pleated in a dry smile. 'Sleep well?'

'Yes, thank you,' she murmured, her throat suddenly dry. Jerkily, she turned her back on him, helping herself to a cup of tea from the pot he'd made.

'You had a phone call last night.'

'Was it the hospital?' Abbey spun round, cup in hand.

Nick shook his head. 'Your friend, Andrea Fraser. I introduced myself, said you'd turned in early. She's invited us out to their place to-day. I accepted. I hope that's all right?'

'It's fine.' Abbey swallowed some of her tea. 'And it'll be nice. I haven't seen the Frasers in a while,' she remarked with a tiny frown. 'You'll like their property, Risden. There's a lovely expanse of river and places to picnic. What time do they want us?'

Nick lifted a shoulder. 'As soon as we'd like. I said we'd need to do a hospital round and so on first.'

'I'll do that.'

'I prefer to check my own post-op patients,' he said evenly.

So, thanks but, no, thanks. Abbey could have let it go but didn't. 'Don't you trust me to know what to look for?'

He made an impatient click with his tongue. 'It's not like we're swamped, Abbey. Lighten up.' He swung to his feet, brushing her arm as he emptied the dregs of his mug into the sink.

She moved away as if she'd been stung, his scathing tone negating any closeness she'd felt towards him last night. She brought her chin up. 'We should arrange an on-call roster, then. I certainly don't want to be treading on your precious toes every time I open my mouth.'

'Now you're being childish,' he said mildly. Dumping his mug in the sink, he walked out.

'I know who's childish!' she flung after him. 'Nick…' She went after him, catching up with him in the hallway opposite his bedroom. 'Why are you being like this?'

He folded his arms, leaning back against the wall and looking big and determined. 'Like what?'

She raised a shoulder uncertainly. 'So… cross.'

'Cross?' The word seemed to amuse him.

Abbey sucked in her breath. 'You know what I mean.' Her gaze steadied on him. The faint shadows under his eyes were obviously a residue of a restless night. Could that mean…? She felt weak suddenly, too near him. 'Didn't you sleep well?'

His shoulders lifted in a long-suffering sigh. 'I slept fine, thanks.' He rubbed a hand through his hair, his mouth compressing on a wry smile. 'I promise I'll be more reasonable after a shower and some breakfast.'

Abbey's thoughts were churning. 'I'll, um, make something, then. I'm quite good at scrambled eggs…'

Several expressions chased through his eyes. 'I know for a fact you're good at any number of things, Dr Jones,' he said, his voice not quite even. 'See you in a bit.'

They left for the Frasers' property just after ten.

'We'll take my car,' Nick said. 'Roads OK?'

'Fine.' Abbey's felt her nerves tighten. Dipping her head, she slid into the passenger seat as he held the door open for her. 'It's about fifty K's out and we'll be travelling in the opposite direction to Jumbuck Ridge,' she told him. 'The country is much more pleasant, softer.'

'So, fill me in about your friends.' Nick was obviously enjoying himself, gunning the Jag along a straight stretch of country road.

'Stuart's a born and bred local. Risden's been in his family for ever. But he's the new-breed grazier. Been away to university and all that stuff. He's a lovely guy. And Andrea and he are just so well suited. Where he's rather considered in what he does, she's all bubbly and spontaneous.'

'Do they have children?' Nick asked interestedly.

'Two. Michael who's eleven and Jazlyn who's nine, I think. They do school at home. Andi was a teacher so she's able to see to all that.'

Nick raised a dark eyebrow. 'How did they meet?'

'Andi was transferred to Wingara Primary. They met at a fundraiser for the hospital.'

For a while then there was silence, until Nick said quietly, 'It really is something special out here, isn't it?' He silenced a self-deprecating laugh, a little amazed at how some inner part of him had begun to respond almost unconsciously to the rich, bold colours of this huge landscape. The true deep blues and rusty reds were stuff from an artist's palette. And the stillness was so intense, he could almost hear his own heartbeat.

'It all kind of takes you over.' Abbey's eyes glowed. 'The landscape seems so pure and clean. And everything seems so incredibly *still*.'

He swung his head towards her and lifted an eyebrow. 'How did you know that's what I was thinking?'

'Just did,' she answered on a half-laugh, and saw a frown notch his forehead. Now what? Was it all right for him to guess her thoughts but not the reverse? Turning her head, she stared out through the side window, her eyes following the distant line of trees that marked the river.

Her thoughts began spinning this way and that. He'd set out deliberately to spend this time with her. Was he now in a way being hoist with his own petard—being made vulnerable by the same physical closeness he'd orchestrated?

The breathtaking thought sent a wild ripple through her veins that powered to a waterfall when his hand reached out, found her fingers and carried them all the way to his lips.

'Well, aren't you the dark horse?' Andrea's blue eyes were alight with conjecture.

'Who, me?' Abbey pretended innocence. She was helping her friend stack the dishwasher after a delicious barbecue lunch of best Risden-produced steaks, potatoes cooked in their jackets in the coals and heaped helpings of salads.

'Yes, you.' A muted 'tsk' left Andrea's mouth. With brisk precision, she slotted the dinner plates into their racks in the dishwasher. 'How long has this been going on?'

Abbey felt warm colour flood her cheeks. 'Nick and I met a few weeks ago in Hopeton—at the TV station of all places. Over a medical debate scheduled for the *Countrywide* programme.'

'Oh, my gosh!' Andrea's hand went to her heart. 'That's brilliant!'

'You wouldn't have thought so if you'd been me,' Abbey said with feeling. 'Anyhow...' she lifted a shoulder expressively '...Nick kind of followed it up.'

'Followed *you* up, you mean!' Andrea was blunt. 'It's obvious something's clicked between you. He can't take his eyes off you. Are you just as keen?'

Abbey groaned. 'Andi, it's early days and it's complicated.'

'He's not married, is he?'

'Of course not!'

'Divorced with dependent children?'

'No!'

'Then, ducky, if you've fallen for him, go for it!' Andrea gave an odd little laugh. 'Not that *I'm* an expert on matters of the heart...'

Abbey looked closely at her friend. All through lunch she'd seemed unlike herself, a bit brittle—especially around her husband. Which was peculiar to say the least. Abbey frowned. Andi and Stuart had always appeared so happy together, their marriage strong...

'OK, that's all done.' Andrea set the cycle, bringing her head up and agitatedly pushing a strand of dark hair away from her face. 'Now, while Stu and the kids are giving Nick the short guided tour of Risden, let's open another bottle of wine and take ourselves out onto the veranda for a while.'

'Um, I'll just have some of your homemade lemonade, thanks, Andi.' Abbey felt a small twinge of unease. Andi was a very moderate drinker at the best of times. But today she'd had several glasses of wine with lunch, and now she was proposing to start on another bottle. But it wasn't Abbey's place to say anything...

'You're giving me your doctor's look.' Andrea's mouth tipped in a crooked smile. 'And you're probably right to stay with the soft stuff. So I'll be good and join you in a lemonade. I've the beginnings of a rotten headache anyway.'

Abbey put her hand on the other's shoulder. 'Can I get you something for it? I brought my bag.'

'I'll take a couple of paracetamol.' Andrea pressed a hand across her eyes. 'And perhaps a cup of tea might be helpful.'

'I'll make it.' Abbey turned to fill the kettle. 'Go and dose yourself and put your feet up. I'll bring the tea out in a jiffy.'

Something was definitely out of kilter here. Two little lines pleated Abbey's forehead as she filled the china teapot and placed two pretty cups and saucers on the tray. Somehow she'd have to get Andrea to open up, because Abbey's trained eye was telling her that her friend was under stress of some kind. She could only hope Andi would let her help.

They sat on the veranda in comfortable old wicker chairs and looked down over the home paddock.

'It's so peaceful here,' Abbey sighed, leaning back in the plump butter-yellow cushions.

'On the surface, yes.' Andrea's throat convulsed as she swallowed. 'I think Stuart's having an affair,' she said in an abrupt way, as if this was what had been simmering in her mind all day.

Abbey's mouth opened and closed. She shook her head. 'That's ridiculous!'

'Is it?' Andrea looked directly at Abbey and her chin lifted defensively. 'We haven't made love in weeks. All he wants to do at night is to sit in front of that bloody computer screen.'

'And that constitutes an affair?' Abbey was in total disbelief. 'Have you asked him what's going on?'

Andrea looked bleak. 'He says he's checking out the market price of beef on the internet.'

'Well, that's feasible, isn't it? It's your livelihood after all.'

'How come he logs off the second I go into his office, then? As though…' Andrea paused and bit her bottom lip. 'As though he's got something to hide?'

Oh, lord. Abbey swung off her chair and went to stand at the railings. She needed to think. Something didn't add up here. Being devious was just not in Stuart's character. Something deeper was happening. She turned her head, her eyes running over her friend's taut face. 'So, are you saying he's *met* someone on the net and it's developed into an online affair?'

Andrea put her cup down carefully on its saucer. 'I know it sounds a bit off the wall for Stuart—but what else could it be?' She palmed the sudden wetness away from her eyes and gave a choked laugh. 'He's certainly gone off me…'

'Honey, that's crazy talk.' Abbey stepped back quickly from the railings, pulling her chair close to the other woman's. She took Andrea's hands and held them firmly. 'It's obvious something is going on with Stu, something he can't talk about. But I'd bet my last dollar he's not been unfaithful—even in cyberspace.'

Andrea's shoulder lifted in a long sigh. 'I'm at my wit's end. That's really why I asked you to come today—I had to talk to someone and I couldn't get into Wingara. It's all been hectic here and the kids have had exams to prepare for—'

'Shh.' Abbey tightened her grip and squeezed. 'I'm glad you called. You and Stu are my friends. And, for whatever reason, I'm always happy to come to this beautiful place, you know that.'

Think. Abbey's troubled gaze left her friend's for a minute and she looked out across the dun-gold grass of the paddocks to the blue-green of the eucalyptuses that lined the stretch of river away in the distance. Suddenly, her fair head came up in query. 'Could Stuart be ill?'

Andrea looked shocked. 'Surely I would've known? I mean, he's still working all the hours God sends…'

'Well, that's what he would do,' Abbey reinforced softly. 'Keep on keeping on, pushing his fears into the background. Pretending everything was normal.'

'Oh, my God…' Andrea's hands came up to press against her cheeks. 'But why wouldn't he have gone to see you? Surely—'

'Andi, listen,' Abbey came in forcefully. 'In the first place, I'm female. Not all men are comfortable with women doctors, especially if it's something highly personal. And in the second, Stu is like every other male in rural Australia. Their health is the last thing they concern themselves with. They're indestructible, as they see it.'

'Could that be it?' Andrea pushed her hair back from her face, pleating a strand as if it helped her think. 'But if he's ill...' Her eyes widened in sudden panic. 'What should I do? Confront him or— Oh, heavens, look! They're back!'

Abbey's gaze swivelled to where the battered Land Rover was coming up the track towards the house. 'Leave it with me,' she counselled quietly. 'Nick's here for a while and he'll be in the surgery each day. Somehow, between us, we'll get Stuart in to see him for a check-up.'

CHAPTER NINE

As it turned out, Abbey found the delicate matter of persuading Stuart to see a doctor was taken right out of her hands.

On their way back to Wingara township, she chatted to Nick about their day. 'Did you enjoy your tour of the place with Stuart?' she asked.

'Immensely. The whole experience has given me a new perspective. Oh, by the way, remind me to have Meri clear a longer than usual appointment time for Wednesday next. Stuart wants a word about a few symptoms he's experiencing.'

Abbey's heart skittered. So her guess had been right. 'Then I hope to heaven he's going to tell Andrea about his appointment with you.'

Nick frowned and then said slowly, 'I didn't realise he'd been keeping things to himself. That's not good.'

'No.' Abbey sighed, letting her head go back on the seat rest. 'She's up the wall with worry—Stuart's begun distancing himself from her emotionally. Andi thinks he's having an affair.'

'Good grief...' Nick muttered, and shook his head.

After a while, Abbey asked, 'Should I say anything to Andi, Nick? I mean, I did point out the possibility that Stuart could be ill—'

'Don't start playing go-between, Abbey.' Nick was firm. 'If you've planted the seed, Andrea can approach her husband. After that it's up to Stuart as to whether or not he wants to open up and express his fears. With the best will in the world, no one, not even his wife, can force him.'

'But that's so infantile!' Abbey exclaimed. 'And so unfair to Andi.'

'Abbey...' Nick warned. 'It'll sort itself out in time.'

Next morning, Abbey went to the surgery early, leaving Nick to do the ward round at the hospital. As she began putting things to rights on her desk, she realised she was on tenterhooks. She'd been hoping with all her heart she would have heard from her friend by now. But Andrea had not been in touch.

Abbey shook her head. Obviously, Stuart hadn't confided in his wife. Instead, he'd probably given her some lame excuse for his trip to town on Wednesday—like having to buy feed for the cattle or go the bank!

Sighing, she moved across to the window of her consulting room and looked out, not registering the beautiful crispness of the morning.

Anxiety for the Frasers' well-being was eating her alive.

She stayed at the window another minute longer and then, determinedly pushing aside her misgivings, returned to her desk, buzzing Meri for her first patient, Rachel Petersen.

'Good morning, Rachel. Are you playing hookey?' Abbey smiled. Rachel was the deputy principal at the primary school.

'I am, actually. But someone's covering for me—at least I hope so.'

Abbey could see at a glance that Rachel was not her usual calm self. She waited until her patient was comfortably seated and then asked, 'So, what can I do for you this morning, Rachel?'

'My hair's falling out.'

Abbey frowned briefly. 'In handfuls or have you just noticed it coming away when you've brushed it?'

The teacher lifted a shoulder. 'It's been a general loss, I suppose—but enough to make me panic. What could be wrong, Abbey?'

'Any number of things.' Abbey was cautious. 'Are you feeling unusually stressed at the moment?'

The woman's shoulders lifted in a heavy sigh. 'Well, as a working single parent, I'm used to keeping all the balls in the air, but just at the moment it's a real effort catching them.

'And teaching is hardly a doddle these days,' she went on ruefully. 'When I first began, it was so much more creative. Now...' She shook her head. 'There are so many rules and regulations. And the calibre of families has changed. For instance, I heard the other day that several of my pupils had been seen foraging from the rubbish bins at the back of the pub. They were hungry, poor little mites, and that's terrible, Abbey! Sorry.' She chewed her lip and gave a wry smile. 'I'm going on and I don't mean to waste your time.'

'You're not.' Abbey was firm. 'But there are two separate issues here, Rachel. First, we'll deal with your health and then I want to hear more about these children. Perhaps if we liaise, something can be done for them. But for the moment, your health is my concern.'

'Well?' Rachel asked a few minutes later, as she pulled herself up from the examination couch and slid her feet to the floor.

'You do appear a little tense.' Abbey said cautiously, washing her hands at the basin. 'And it may be just a case of everything catching up with you and depleting your energy stores, both physically and mentally. But in view of your hair loss, we'll run a check to rule out any thyroid imbalance.'

'How will you do that?' Rachel slipped her shoes back on and took her place back at Abbey's desk.

'A blood test is the most accurate. If your thyroid is under-active, it can certainly cause premature hair loss. Fortunately, simple re-placement medication can soon put things right.'

Rachel's hands interlocked on the desktop. 'And if it's not that causing the hair loss?'

Abbey heard the thread of anxiety in her pa-tient's voice and sought to reassure her. 'There are several options we can try. A multimineral tablet containing zinc can be helpful and there've been good results from a new lotion that can be rubbed into your scalp to help hair growth. Of course, don't neglect the obvious.' Abbey smiled. 'Regular shampooing and mas-sage.'

'Massage…' Rachel managed a wry smile. 'That sounds like a recipe for relaxation.'

'We'll start with the lotion while we're wait-ing for the result of your blood test to come back.' Abbey pulled her pad towards her. 'And you'd probably benefit from some actual re-laxation therapy.' She looked up, her eyebrows raised in query. 'Isn't something happening at the sports centre along those lines?'

'We received some flyers at the school about it.' Rachel looked uncertain. 'I could perhaps try that, couldn't I?'

'Absolutely.' Abbey smiled. She handed the prescription across. 'Now, I'll take some blood and while I'm doing that, you can tell me about these children.'

When her last patient for the morning had gone, Abbey sat on at her desk, her head low-ered, her fingers gently massaging her temples.

It had been one of those mornings when she'd been expected to be all things to all peo-ple. She sighed, considering her own emo-tional state.

Everything always came back to Nick Tonnelli—large as life, a man waiting for some kind of sign from her that they could move forward. But to where? And to what? Abbey made a little sound of frustration, suddenly at odds with the emotional games people were forced to play.

She looked up as a rap sounded on her door.

'Come in.' Abbey hurriedly schooled her expression.

'Got a minute?' Nick's dark head came through the opening.

'If you've come bearing coffee, I've probably got several.' Abbey forced a wry smile and brought her gaze up to meet his.

'Ah...' Nick looked rueful. 'I've already had some. Could I—?'

'No, it's OK.' Abbey waved him in. 'I'm just feeling the aftermath of a heavy morning. I'll buzz Meri to bring some. Could you manage another?'

Nick shrugged. 'If Meri doesn't mind.'

'Of course not,' Abbey said dismissively. 'We look after each other here.' Reaching out, she pressed a button on the intercom.

'Tough list?' Nick parked himself in the chair opposite her.

'I'm not complaining.' In a nervous gesture, Abbey caught up her hair from her collar and let it go, for the first time noticing he was carrying a patient file.

'Stuart Fraser doesn't seem to have much of a medical history with us.' Nick tossed the notes to one side and sent her a quizzical look.

'He probably doesn't.' Abbey shrugged. 'I think I've only seen him once, when he needed a tetanus jab. In the past he may have seen Wolf.'

'Obviously just for routine stuff,' Nick said. 'Minor farm accidents and so on.'

'Here we are!' Meri announced cheerfully, as she arrived with a pot of coffee and a plate of chocolate biscuits. 'Energy hit for you. And I'd guess much needed. Patients coming out of the woodwork this morning,' she lamented. 'But probably half of them only came to get a look at Nick.'

'They don't still do that, do they?'

'With bells on.' Abbey felt a bubble of laughter rise in her chest at his look of disbelief. 'Thanks, Meri.' She sent the receptionist a warm smile. 'This will really hit the spot.'

'You're welcome,' Meri responded cheerfully, and turned to leave. 'Oh, Nick…' She paused at the door. 'Some emails have come through for you.'

'Excellent. I wasn't expecting to hear back so promptly.'

'I'll print them out and leave them on your desk,' Meri offered obligingly, fluttering a wave as she left.

'I shot off a couple this morning to colleagues in Sydney,' Nick explained, spinning his hands up behind his neck. 'I want to cover all the bases before I see Stuart.'

Abbey felt her stomach twist at the implication. 'What do you suspect?'

'Prostate.'

'He's only forty-two.'

Nick looked tensely back behind her to the startling brilliance of blue sky. 'And his father died of prostate cancer at sixty-eight.'

'Oh, lord.' Abbey closed her eyes for a second and then opened them, staring down at her hands clasped on her lap. She looked up, her eyes meeting Nick's with a plea. 'If Stuart has prostate cancer, what are his options? From my knowledge, they're few and fairly radical.'

'Abbey, don't go there, all right?' Nick's eyebrows jumped together in sudden irritation. 'At least, not yet. We'll know more on Wednesday after Stuart's been in.' His mouth tightened. 'I urged him to come and see me this morning, practically pleaded with him. But apparently he had to do something with his bloody cows!'

'Stu's a farmer, Nick,' Abbey explained patiently. 'His cows will always come first. And you beating yourself up for not persuading him to come in immediately won't change his mindset. By the way, he's booked for eleven o'clock.'

At fifteen minutes to eleven on Wednesday, Meri rang through from Reception. 'You've no one else booked for today, Abbey, but Andrea Fraser's here with her husband. He's just gone in to see Nick and she wondered if you'd have time for a word.'

'Of course.' Abbey's mind flew into over-drive. 'I'll be right out, Meri.' Her hand shaking, she put the receiver down, a new foreboding shadowing her thoughts.

She found Andrea standing stiffly beside the reception counter, her face pinched-looking, her hair uncombed and sticking out at odd angles, as though her appearance had been the last thing on her mind when she'd left home. Abbey looped a comforting arm around her friend's shoulders. 'Let's go out onto the back deck where we can talk,' she said quietly.

'He told me this morning,' Andrea said without preamble, shredding the tissue she was winding in and out of her fingers. 'It's his prostate for sure. He hasn't been able to pee properly.' Tears suddenly welled in her eyes. 'The awful part is his dad died from prostate cancer.' She stopped and took a shuddering breath. 'Stuart's been sick with worry and that's what he's been doing on the net, trying to find out about the symptoms and treatment. Oh, Abbey…I don't know what I'd do if anything happened to Stu…'

'Andi, you're getting way ahead of yourself,' Abbey cautioned firmly. 'Self-diagnosis is a dangerous thing. We have to wait for Nick. But in view of his family history, Stuart is right to seek medical help. Difficulty in passing urine is the first symptom something is amiss.'

Andrea's eyes widened momentarily in apprehension. 'What will Nick do first, then? And what will he be looking for?'

'He'll do a physical examination, which will tell him if the prostate gland is enlarged.'

Andrea shook her head. 'It's all such gobbledegook. I mean, I don't even know exactly where the prostate *is,* for heaven's sake!'

'The prostate gland is about the size of a walnut and it's situated at the base of the bladder,' Abbey explained gently. 'So, of course, when it begins to enlarge, as it seems to have done in Stu's case, it puts pressure on the urethra. That's the clinical name for the urine-carrying tube.'

'It's very much a male thing, isn't it?'

'Yes.'

'Oh, lord, Abbey.' Andrea laughed, a strange little tragic sound. 'What if he—if we can't ever—'

'Stop it, Andi.' Abbey homed in exactly on her friend's scrambled thoughts. 'Your mind's running too far ahead.'

Andrea dabbed at her eyes. 'C-can you blame me?'

'No, of course not. Stuart has always been well and strong. It comes as a great shock to any of us when illness suddenly makes us vulnerable. But come on, now,' she said bracingly. 'Let's cheer up. I have a feeling Nick will want to speak to you and Stuart together after he's done Stu's medical.'

'I should fix myself up a bit, then.' Andrea gave a shaky smile. 'I don't remember whether I even washed my face this morning. And my hair must look like it's been shoved in the microwave.'

'Well, Doc, what do you reckon?' Stuart began zipping up his trousers.

'First things first, Stuart.' Nick stripped off his gloves and went to wash his hands. 'As a matter of urgency, we need to get your urine moving again.'

'Tell me about it.' Stuart sank wearily into his chair. 'What do I have to do?'

Nick's mouth clamped as he took his place back at the desk. 'It's more what I have to do, mate. But I think you'd be more comfortable over at the hospital for the procedure.'

'You mean you have to cut me?' Stuart looked alarmed.

'No surgery.' Nick shook his head. 'Not at the moment anyway. But for starters I'll have to do some fancy stuff with a flexible tube to drain your bladder.' His dark head bent, Nick scribbled something on Stuart's card. 'How would you be placed to make an immediate trip to Sydney?'

Stuart's eyes clouded. 'How immediate?'

'Tomorrow?'

'I'd have to think about it, Doc.'

'Stuart, we can't wait on this.' Nick was frank. 'You need to be under the care of a urologist. I'd willingly stay as your doctor but it's not my field.'

Stuart chewed on his bottom lip. 'Could I maybe see someone in Hopeton?'

Nick lifted a shoulder. 'You could, but the regular guy isn't due to take a clinic until next month.'

'And that's not soon enough?'

'Not from my information, no.' There was moment of intense silence and a creak of leather as Nick leaned back in his chair and steepled his fingers under his chin. 'To begin with, the specialist will want to do an ultrasound of your prostate or a biopsy or both. He'll follow this up with a PSA—a diagnostic prostate-specific antigen blood test.'

''Struth!' Stuart's large hand clenched on the desktop. 'Now you're sounding like the vet around one of my cows.' He gave Nick a very straight look. 'Does all this stuff have to be done because of my dad's history?'

'It would be remiss of me not to refer you.' Nick was guarded. 'Do you have brothers?'

'One. He lives in Hopeton.'

'Then he should get himself along to his doctor and have this test done as well.'

Stuart looked shell-shocked, as if the seriousness of his situation had just begun to sink in. 'I've a wife and two young kids, Nick.' His throat jerked as he swallowed. 'If I've got it—the big C, I mean—what are my chances?'

Nick's mouth pursed thoughtfully. 'No one's going to rush you into anything, Stuart. And if you're comparing your situation with your father's, don't. You told me he was in his late sixties when he was diagnosed and the cancer spread swiftly. You're a much younger man and you'll have options your dad didn't have. But look...' Nick spread his hands across the desktop '...don't let's jump the gun. Let's just get you over to the hospital and made more comfortable for a start.' He glanced at his watch. 'But first we'd better get Andi in here and tell her briefly what's going on. Then I suggest we schedule a proper talk for a bit later on today. Suit you?'

'Guess so.' Stuart rubbed a knuckled hand along his jaw, sending Nick a beseeching blue look. 'Does she have to know everything?'

Nick swung out of his chair and crossed to his patient's side, propping himself on the edge of the desk. 'I understand you want to protect your wife, Stu, but for both your sakes, Andrea needs to know what's going on. Besides...' Nick's mouth crimped at the corners in a dry grin '...Abbey would skin me alive if I let you off.'

Later that afternoon arrangements for the Frasers were discussed and clarified. And then things began moving swiftly.

As it was the larger of the two, they'd all gathered in Abbey's consulting room.

'OK.' Nick opened Stuart's file and began to refer to it. 'I've got you in to see James Ferguson on Friday morning, nine o'clock, Stuart. Is that going to give you enough time to get to Sydney and settle in?'

Stuart looked at his wife. 'Should do, shouldn't it?'

'We fly out on the noon plane from Hopeton tomorrow and it's only an hour's flight so, yes, that sounds good, Nick.'

'What about the children?' Abbey asked.

'Oh, we'll take them with us.' Andrea was unequivocal. 'We need to stay together as a family through this.' She sent a brave little smile around the assembled company. 'Don't we, Stu?'

For answer, Stuart reached across and took his wife's hand, bringing it across to rest on his thigh. 'This Ferguson chap, Nick...' Stuart looked uncertain. 'He won't be all stiff and starchy, will he?'

'Not at all.' Nick's pose was relaxed as he leaned back in his chair and folded his arms. 'I play squash with him. He's about your age, wife and kids. Laid-back kind of guy. You'll find him easy to talk to.'

'How did you get us in so quickly?' Andrea still looked a little bemused at the speed with which everything had been arranged. 'I mean, sometimes it takes months to see a specialist.'

Nick's hand moved dismissively. 'We exchange favours from time to time. It's no big deal.'

Andrea dropped her gaze. 'I thought perhaps Stu's case was desperately urgent or something...'

'It is in a way,' Abbey came in guardedly. 'For your peace of mind, you both need to know what's going on, rather than waiting in limbo until Stuart can be seen some time in the future. Wouldn't you agree?'

The Frasers' nods of agreement synchronised and they clasped their hands more tightly. 'Thanks, both of you.' Andrea's voice came out huskily and she bit her lips. 'And thank God you were here for my man, Nick— that's all I can say.'

'Fair go, love,' Stuart protested mildly. 'I would've got my act together eventually and consulted Abbey. I was just...'

'Chicken?' supplied his wife with a grin.

Everyone laughed, breaking the tense nature of the consultation.

'Well, if that's all you need us for, I think we'll get home.' Andrea looked expectantly at her husband who nodded and looked relieved that the taxing day was almost over.

'Right. Here's your letter of referral.' Nick handed the long white envelope over to his patient. 'I'll email Jim anyway so he'll have your history in advance. And we'll be in touch, Stu, when you get back.'

'You betcha.' Stuart held out his hand. 'Thanks, Nick. I don't know what else to say. And, Abbey…' His face worked for a minute. 'Thanks for the support. You don't know how much it means to us…'

When they'd seen the Frasers out, Nick closed the door and stood against it. He lifted his gaze and looked straight at Abbey.

Her mouth opened on a little breath of sound, glimpsing something in the sea-green depths of his eyes that alarmed her. 'You're worried, aren't you?'

Nick's mouth tightened. 'It shows, huh?' He shovelled both hands through his hair, moving across to stand with his back against the window-ledge.

'What did you find?' Abbey felt a curl of unease.

'Enough to wish Stuart had got himself checked out long before this.'

'Oh, no…' She sank down on the edge of the desk. Everything Nick was saying indicated that Stuart and Andrea could be facing some agonising decisions. 'Traditionally, we were taught that prostate cancer was a tortoise,' she said bleakly. 'So slow-growing that something else was likely to kill a man off first. Now…' She stopped and shook her head.

'Now we find it's a whole new ball game,' Nick picked up flatly. 'Traditional thinking is out the window. Heart attacks and strokes have lost some of their first-strike capacity and prostate cancer is right up there as a possible killer.'

Abbey's throat lumped. 'If it's bad news, how are the Frasers going to cope?'

Nick returned her stricken look without flinching. 'They'll cope, Abbey. They'll have to. And we'll do everything we can to support them.'

'We shouldn't pre-empt the outcome of the tests, though,' she pointed out logically, clinging to the thread of hope.

Nick's mouth compressed into a straight line. 'We could be more optimistic if the father's medical history wasn't staring us in the face.'

Sweet heaven. Abbey tamped down the sudden dread in her heart. 'Poor Andi and Stu,' she said faintly. 'It makes you realise just how tenuous life is. How precious.'

'Hell, yes.' Nick sent her a searching look and felt a fullness in his heart he couldn't deny. Almost defensively, as if he needed to hide his emotions, he turned away and looked out of the window. A beat of silence. 'Did you have anything planned for the rest of the day?' he threw back over his shoulder.

Abbey looked blank for a moment and then rallied. 'I have a meeting over at the school. It seems we have a batch of ''new poor'' in Wingara—families who through no fault of their own are finding life very difficult.'

'Surely that's a matter for the social security people?'

'More often than not, it's the long way round a problem,' she pointed out with a sigh.

'Where possible, we prefer to handle things like this on a community level. And with that in mind, the deputy principal is liaising with several relevant organisations and yours truly to try to see if we can get a breakfast group going at the school, feed any child who's hungry for one reason or another.' Abbey stopped, her teeth biting into the softness of her lower lip reflectively. 'Although getting someone to run it might be a problem. Everyone's so busy with their own lives these days.'

'Mmm…'

Abbey looked at him sharply. Had he heard anything she'd said? His attention seemed to have dissipated like leaves in the wind. She straightened off the edge of the desk and stood upright. 'What about you?' she asked, taking the few paces to join him at the window.

He drew in a deep breath that came out as a ragged sigh. 'If you don't need me for anything, I think I'll go for a long run, slough off some of this gloom. After sending Stuart off to face who knows what, I feel carved up inside.'

'Oh, Nick...' She shook her head in slight disbelief. Nicholas Tonnelli feeling vulnerable? How wrong could you be about people? She'd had no idea the Frasers' situation would have got to him like this. With his kind of professional experience, she would have thought he'd have had objectivity down to a fine art—be, at the very least, case-hardened.

He gave a huff of raw laughter. 'Pathetic, isn't it?'

'No, it's not,' she came back softly. 'It's just being human.' She took a tentative step towards him. 'How can I help?'

'Just let me hold you.'

Her heart gave an extra thud. 'A medicinal hug?'

'Yes, please, Doctor.' Wearing a faintly twisted smile, Nick drew her unresisting body against his.

Pressed against the hardness of him, Abbey made a little sound in her throat, the clean familiarity of his scent surrounding her. After a long time, she pulled back and said shakily, 'I...should get to my meeting.'

'Should you?' His dark head swooped towards her, his mouth teasingly urgent against her lips, the corner of her mouth. 'Off you go, then,' he said, regret in his gruffness. 'I'll come out and see you off.'

They walked out to Reception together. 'Mind how you go.' Opening the outer door, he ushered her through.

Abbey sent him an old-fashioned look. 'I'll be sure to watch out for the teeming masses at the intersection. Enjoy your run.'

Nick's eyes glinted with dry humour. Propping himself against the doorframe, he watched her drive off with a fluttered wave in his direction. He huffed a frustrated sigh as he turned back inside. Hell, he was missing her already.

Wandering through to his room, he collected his bag and set the alarm. Was it possible to fast-track love? It must be. He certainly had a king-sized dose of it!

'Abbey...' He said her name softly. Already she'd stirred such powerful feelings in him, imbued him with a zest for the ordinary things of life, the precious, simple things that he'd all but forgotten.

CHAPTER TEN

AT THE meeting, Abbey tried to pay attention. But every now and again she was conscious of her thoughts wandering, becoming way too fanciful for comfort.

Was she in love with Nicholas Tonnelli? Colour whipped along her cheekbones at the mere thought. Was this how it felt—wild for the sight of him, the touch of him? Merely thinking about the possibility made her remember the night he'd massaged her feet. The night he'd carried her to bed...

Dreamily, she propped her chin on her hand. Just recalling the way they'd batted the loaded suggestions back and forth was doing crazy things to her insides, fuelling the slow crawl of nerves in her stomach—

'What do you think, Abbey? Feasible?'

'Uh...' Abbey snapped back to reality, surveying the expectant faces of the newly formed committee around her. She'd heard Rachel Petersen's voice but her question had become lost in the fog of Abbey's introspection. Hastily, she picked up her pen and twirled it, gaining time. 'Just run that past me again.'

Rachel raised a finely etched eyebrow. 'Are you OK, Abbey? You look a bit hot.' She gave a 'tsk' of irritation. 'It's probably this blessed air-conditioning again. It's never been adjusted properly.'

'I'm fine.' Abbey took a mouthful from the glass of water in front of her. 'Just a bit of a headache starting.' She drummed up a quick smile. 'You were saying?'

'I suggested we use the facilities at the school tuck shop for this breakfast club. It's just had a major revamp and, as it's on school property, we could keep an eye on things.'

'It sounds ideal.' Abbey linked the assembled group with a questioning look. 'If everyone is happy about that?'

Sounds of agreement echoed around the table. 'What kind of tucker would you suggest we serve the kiddies?' Geoff Rogers asked

practically. 'It's winter now. Poor little blight-
ers need something to warm their insides.'

'Porridge?' Fran, Geoff's wife, suggested.

'Not all kids like porridge,' Abbey said
thoughtfully. 'But, of course, we could still offer it. Perhaps cereal and warm milk? Toast
with a nourishing spread?'

'I'm sure we could manage fruit when so
much is grown locally.' Rachel's voice bub-
bled with enthusiasm. 'We could even run to
grilled tomatoes or scrambled eggs.'

'And what about a nice thick vegetable soup
at lunchtime?' Fran suggested. 'Then, if the
parents can't provide much for supper, at least
the little ones will have something in their
tummies.'

'It's not just the poorer families of the town
who need the facility,' Rachel said earnestly.
'Some of the children who come on buses
from the outlying districts have to leave home
very early. I'm sure half of them aren't up to
eating much breakfast, even if it's put in front
of them. But by the time they get here to
school, they're ravenous.'

'How are we going to judge numbers, then?' One of the members of the P and C committee came in for the first time.

'I do have some knowledge of this kind of venture from an inner-city practice where I worked once,' Abbey said, and realised every- one was looking speculatively at her. 'We may err on the side of ordering too much at first but things usually even out after a while. And basically...' she rocked a hand expressively '...if the leftovers are stored properly, there won't be much loss.'

'There's just one tiny thing.' Rachel sent a hopeful look around the table. 'Who's going to run it? We need someone who's used to catering for numbers but who can order eco- nomically at the same time. Funding is avail- able but we certainly can't waste it.'

There was a beat of silence while everyone thought, and then the obvious solution hit Abbey like a bolt of lightning. Looking pleased, she snapped her diary shut. 'What about Ed Carmichael?'

There was a momentary hush. And then a babble of excited voices. 'I must say, I'd always thought in terms of a woman running the scheme.' Geoff stroked his chin thoughtfully. 'But crikey! Ed's a natural when you think about it. He's been a camp cook for the shearers. And there's no doubt we could rely on him to do the right thing by the kids.'

'I often see him around the town.' Someone else sought to have their say. 'He always looks very neat and clean.'

'And I know Ed would do a wonderful job.' Abbey's eyes were lit with warmth. 'Plus I'm almost sure he'd want to give this service to the children on a voluntary basis.'

There were smiles of satisfaction and little nods of approval. 'I'll approach Mr Carmichael officially, then.' Rachel positively beamed. 'We could have our children eating properly within a matter of hours. Thank you, everyone, for coming. A most gratifying result.'

Abbey drove home slowly. It was almost dusk and she wondered whether Nick was back from his run. Her stomach tightened. She *needed* him to be back, she realised with a little jolt. Switching off the engine, she climbed out of her vehicle and went into the house by the back door.

A wonderful aroma drifted out from the kitchen. 'Nick?' She walked quickly through the laundry, not believing the joy she felt. He was planted firmly at the stove, cooking.

'Hi.' He turned his head as she came through and they shared a tentative smile. 'Good meeting?'

Abbey nodded. 'Very productive. Looks like you've been productive as well. What are you making?'

'Vegetable curry.' He went back to his stirring. 'I'll do the rice now you're home.'

Home. Abbey's heart slammed against her ribs. If only she and Nick were sharing a real home together. As a couple. In love…

'Oh—OK. I'll just, um, get a shower, then.' Heart pounding, she slipped past him, her thoughts whirling. So what am I going to do about you, Nick? she fretted, stripping off her work clothes and stepping under the jets of warm water.

'Oh, lord,' she whispered, feelings of apprehension rushing at her. How could this have happened? In so short a time and with her hardly realising it, she'd come to depend on him so much. In all the ways that counted. But he had a life in Sydney. A life in the fast lane.

A life she could never be a part of.

The week dragged to a close.

On Friday at four o'clock, Nick poked his head into Abbey's consulting room. 'I'm off to do a ward round.'

'Fine,' she responded dispiritedly. She'd been hoping against hope there would have been some word from Andrea by now. But apart from James Ferguson's brief advice to Nick that Stuart had been seen and that the specialist had put a rush on the test results, there'd been nothing.

'It's too soon to have heard anything definite, Abbey.' Nick homed in on her worries accurately. He came in and closed the door.

'I know.' She lifted a shoulder. 'Are you releasing Grant today?'

'I thought so, yes. He's made a very quick recovery.' Nick parked himself on the corner of her desk. 'I've begun liaising with Fran Rogers about some physio for him. I gather she's already been in for a chat and told Grant what he can expect by way of rehab.' He arched an eyebrow. 'What's the status of the flu jabs for Wingara's senior population?'

'Down on last year.' Abbey looked taken aback at his abrupt change of conversation. 'Why do you ask?'

'There's been a procession of elderly folk going down with flu right throughout the district, according to Rhys and Diane. Some are being cared for at home by their relatives, but the hospital's receiving its fair share of patients as well.'

Abbey dropped her gaze. Nick had placed himself on ward rounds for the entire week so she hadn't been near the hospital.

'Ideally, they should all have had their flu vaccinations way back.' Nick spun off the desk and paced to the window. Turning, he folded his arms and frowned. 'What kind of preventative campaign did you run?'

Abbey's chin came up. What did he think she was running here, the World Health Organisation? And surely he wasn't blaming her for people's failure to take responsibility for their own health? 'We had the usual reminders around the surgery and I put a piece in the local paper advising folk that the vaccine was here and it was time to get their shots,' she snapped defensively. 'It's up to individuals, Nick. It's not as though they can be corralled like cows and given a jab.'

His dark brows drew together. 'I'm not so far removed from grassroots medicine that I'm unaware of that, Abbey. But perhaps it's time to think ahead and see what we could do for next year.'

Next year? Abbey felt as if all her muscle supports had suddenly let go. Where was Nick Tonnelli coming from? He wouldn't be here next *month*—let alone next year!

'What did you have in mind?' she asked in a tone of controlled patience.

He took a few steps to spin out a chair and drop into it, leaning forward earnestly. 'I thought I'd have a word with Rob Stanton, get a couple of his documentary team out here.'

'In what capacity?'

'We could film a segment for the *Country-wide* programme.' Nick's gaze lit up with the enthusiasm of his plan. 'Feature several of the locals who have come down with flu, speak to them now, when they're recovering, and have them recount how debilitated they've felt and how they'll be sure to have their flu shots in future. We could get Rob to put it to air—say, March, April next year. What do you think?'

Abbey had to admit the idea had merit but nevertheless voiced her reservations. 'People may not want cameras and microphones in their faces, though.'

'Naturally, we'd need their permission.' Nick remained undaunted. 'But I'm sure Rob would do a sensitive, folksy piece that would have the right amount of impact. And he certainly owes you big time for that business over the debate,' he ended darkly.

Abbey avoided his eyes, her mouth trembling infinitesimally at the mention of that particular day. The day her life had been altered for ever. 'All right.' She picked up the phone as it rang beside her. 'But I want to see the film clip before it goes to air. I don't want any of my patients being made to look like yokels. If Rob can work with that…'

Nick shrugged. 'I'll run the idea past him and get back to you.'

They did the grocery shopping on Saturday afternoon, bickering lightly over the menu for the coming week. 'We could have a cooking session tomorrow,' Abbey suggested, stopping by the meat cabinet. 'Cook enough food for the week and store it in the freezer.'

'Not on your life!' Nick's mouth turned down. 'I've got more to do with my Sunday that spend it in the kitchen, thank you.' Gently, he prised her fingers off the large tray of beef cuts.

'Nick!' She grabbed his hand to stop him and was startled by the wild shiver of electricity that ran between them. Flustered, she met his eyes and saw an answering flare before he doused it.

'Let's have a picnic tomorrow instead,' he suggested, his voice slightly uneven. 'I'll grab a couple of these T-bone steaks. We could find a spot by the river and barbecue them. How does that sound?'

Abbey's heart wrenched. It sounded wonderful.

By mid-week, Abbey was beginning to feel that as far as the Frasers were concerned, no news was definitely not good news. And when Nick took a phone call during their lunch-break and didn't return, her nerves began gathering and clenching like fine wires.

She glanced at her watch. Heavens, he'd been gone for ages. Hastily, she rinsed the crockery they'd used for their simple snack and then, as if compelled by forces outside herself, went along to his consulting room and knocked.

'Come in and close the door, Abbey.' Nick looked back from his stance at the window and beckoned her inside. He pulled a couple of chairs together and they sat facing one another. Silently, he reached out and took her hands, rubbing his thumbs almost absently over her knuckles. 'I'm afraid it's not good news about Stuart.'

Her mouth dried. 'Was that Dr Ferguson on the phone?'

'Yes. Stuart's been advised to undergo a radical prostatectomy.'

Abbey paled and whispered. 'Oh, no...'

'Jim called in a second opinion, Magnus Nahrung from the Prince Alfred. He agreed with Jim's findings.'

'When will they do the surgery?'

'He's down for tomorrow morning.' At Abbey's little gasp, Nick continued flatly, 'Apparently, Stu didn't want to hang about.'

Abbey was aghast. 'He could be left impotent, Nick!'

'Or dead within ten years if the cancer gets into his bones and he doesn't have the surgery.' Nick's response was brutally frank. 'Optimistic inaction certainly isn't an option. And whatever it takes, Stuart wants to stay with his family, Abbey. He told me that much.'

Abbey took a shaken breath. 'Have they had counselling? Of course they have…' She grimaced, answering her own question. She swallowed the tears clogging her throat. 'Did Dr Ferguson say how Stuart and Andi are handling things?'

Nick allowed himself a lopsided smile. 'With amazing calm and stoicism, he said. Whatever their own misgivings, they're putting a positive spin on things for the kids' sakes.'

Abbey bit her lip. 'That sounds like them, doesn't it?' She spun up off the chair, wrapping her arms around her midriff. 'I wonder why Andi hasn't called?'

'She'll have all her thoughts focused on her husband at the moment, Abbey. Frankly, outside the hospital staff, I doubt she'd have the energy to talk to anyone right now. But she'll know our thoughts are with her and Stuart.'

'Yes.' Abbey swallowed hard and nodded. 'Yes, she will...'

That night, Abbey woke from a dream with her heart pounding and a scream in her throat.

In seconds Nick was in the doorway. 'Abbey—what's up? Are you ill?'

She sat upright and snapped the bedside lamp on. 'I must've had a bad dream.'

'More like a nightmare.' Nick's voice was gruff and he came further into the room.

Abbey pushed a strand of hair away from her face. 'It was about Andi and Stuart...'

'You're trembling.' The mattress gave under his weight, and then his arms were around her, cradling her against his chest. 'You can't let it get to you like this,' he murmured throatily. 'What happened to objectivity?'

'Pie in the sky.' Abbey gave a shuddery little breath, snuggling into the hollow of his shoulder. 'You haven't been to bed,' she said, feeling the soft stuff of the track top he'd put on earlier, after his shower.

He gave a hard laugh. 'I'm too wired to sleep. Stuart's been on my mind, too.'

'What happened to objectivity?' She brought a hand up and stroked his face, loving the smooth sweep of his skin against her palm.

'Out with the bath water.'

'We're a fine pair, aren't we?' She smoothed back his eyebrow with the side of her thumb. 'What've you been doing?'

'I tried to read. Ended up watching a late movie on TV.' His arms tightened. 'Try to get back to sleep now, OK?'

'I don't think I can,' she sighed. Beside which, his scent was too disturbing. So was the warmth of his body against hers.

'What should we do, then?' His voice was low, deeper than deep. It sought out hidden nerve ends, whispered along blood vessels and right into her heart.

'We could make some cocoa,' she said throatily.

'I hate cocoa.'

Abbey could hardly breathe, arching against him as strong fingers touched where she so longed to be touched. 'Bedtime story?'

'Mmm. About a man and a woman...' he said huskily, drawing her to her feet.

Safe in his arms, Abbey closed her eyes, feeling every sense spring alive, the drugging drift of the sandalwood soap on his skin swirling around her like so many strands of silk.

Her hands, with a mind of their own, smoothed over him, from the hardness of his shoulder muscles to curve lower, then round by the hollow of his hip, then on, dragging a primitive groan from his throat.

'Abbey—enough!'

'I'm sorry...' Stung by the reprimand, she pulled back, inflamed by the response of her own body.

'God, no! That's not what I meant.' Nick spoke as if the air was being pushed out of his body. Tipping her face up, he stared down into her eyes. 'I want you,' he said deeply. 'I think you're wonderful. And beautiful. And perfect...'

'I'm not perfect,' she countered softly, her hair glinting silver in the lamplight as she shook her head.

'Perfect for me...' With a long shudder, he dragged air into his lungs. 'Do you want me as much as I want you?'

Drawn by something in his voice, her gaze came up slowly, meeting such a naked look of longing it took her breath away. Desire, fierce and unrelenting, tore through her, annihilating at a stroke any doubts she might have had.

'Don't you have too many clothes on?' Her huff of laughter was fractured, nerves gripping her insides like tentacles.

With fingers that were not quite steady, he slid the lacy strap of her nightie off her shoulder. 'I wondered when you'd notice.'

Abbey took a shaken breath, held captive by the look in his eyes. The first touch of his mouth on hers shattered the last slender threads of her control as he gathered her in.

Their clothes seemed to fall away.

He's beautiful. Abbey's breath lodged in her throat. Strong, lean, powerful, the sprinkle of dark hair tangling across the centre of his chest, arrowing down...

In the warm glow of the lamplight, she touched him, her fingertips sensitised as they travelled over his body, his gasp of pleasure fuelling her own desire.

And then it was Nick's turn. Using his hands like a maestro, he raised her awareness to fever pitch, his lips following with a devastating intimacy that left her reeling, a jangle of senses, of touch and taste and feeling.

When they arrived at the moment when all was trust, she looked right into his eyes, the moment so tender, so precious. 'Sweet Abbey,' she heard him whisper, before they closed their eyes and the pleasure of giving and receiving claimed them, the intensity whirling them under and then as they reached flashpoint, rolling in long, flowing waves to envelop them.

Afterwards, they lay for a long time just holding each other. Abbey could hardly believe it.

She'd become Nick Tonnelli's lover. Oh, lord, she thought.

She must have spoken the exclamation aloud for Nick frowned suddenly. 'Not regretting anything, are you, Abbey?' Lifting his head slightly, he smudged a kiss over her temple. 'It was beautiful—wasn't it?'

'Beautiful,' she echoed. There was no point in saying otherwise. It would have been a lie. But what in real terms did being lovers mean? And where did they go from here? Abbey closed her eyes, her face warm against his naked chest. 'Nick...' Her voice was hesitant. 'We, um, didn't use anything.'

He went still. 'I assumed—expected you to say something if it wasn't all right.'

She placed a finger across his lips. It probably was all right. She was as regular as clockwork. 'It should be OK. I'm in a safe time.'

Not two minutes later the phone rang. Nick swore. 'Stay there—I'll get it.' He reached for his track pants and dragged them on. He wasn't away long.

'Well?' Struggling upright, Abbey pulled the sheet up to her chin.

'MVA, sole occupant. ETA ten minutes. Doesn't sound too serious. I'll handle it. Curl up now and try to get some sleep, OK?'

She took an uncertain breath. 'Yes...all right. Mind how you go.'

He leaned over and knuckled her cheek. 'Always do.'

Not always, Nick. The sobering little thought stayed with Abbey until she finally fell into a dreamless sleep.

Next morning she was up and dressed and in the surgery before Nick had even surfaced. Her excuse was that she had paperwork to get up to date, scripts to write...

She worked for nearly an hour and then put her pen down. She'd have to see Nick the moment he got in. At the thought of what she had to ask him, her stomach somersaulted. And when, shortly after, she heard his steady footfall outside in the corridor, the soft closing of his surgery door, her heartbeat quickened alarmingly, almost choking her.

The walk to his consulting room seemed endless. She paused for a moment outside his door then, taking a deep breath, she knocked and went in.

'Abbey…' Nick wanted to spring from his chair and gather her in but something in her expression held him back. 'Meri said you'd left a note not to be disturbed.'

'Reams of paperwork to catch up on.' She gave the semblance of a smile. 'How was your MVA?'

Nick made a dismissive movement with his hand. 'Suspected drunk driver. Silly young kid still on his provisional licence. Geoff Rogers wanted a blood alcohol reading.'

'Much damage?' Immediately Abbey's caring instincts were aroused.

'Whiplash, gash to his head. I've just been over to check on him. He's a bit sick and sorry for himself. It's to be hoped he's learned his lesson about drinking and driving.' Abruptly, Nick stood to his feet, his eyes raking her face. 'Are you OK?'

'Fine,' she lied. 'I just need you to—that is, I wondered if you'd mind signing this.' She slid her hand into the side pocket of her skirt and withdrew a slip of paper. 'It's a script,' she elaborated, handing it across to him.

'Yes, I can see that.' He frowned down at the computer printout. 'It's made out to you.'

She gave a strangled laugh. 'It's not ethical to sign one's own prescription, Nick. You must know that.'

'It's for the morning-after pill.' His voice had risen and tightened. He looked up, his eyes unguarded. 'Why, Abbey?'

Thoughts, all of them confused, clawed at her. 'Because I don't want to take any chances,' she said wretchedly.

'You said you were safe.' He dropped back into his chair, as if his strings had been cut.

'I'm as sure as I can be that I'm safe, but who can ever be that sure? I mean, we're both fit and healthy. There's every reason to think we could...' She stopped and faced him with uncertainty and wariness clouding her eyes.

Nick felt something cold run down his back-bone. He flicked at the piece of paper in his hand. 'Are you sure you want to go this road, Abbey? I mean, if we've made a baby to-gether—'

She interrupted him with a humourless little laugh. 'Nick, you're a free spirit. You don't want a baby. You like the unencumbered life-style you've chosen, otherwise you'd have changed it long ago.'

His dark brows shot together. 'Don't pre-sume to know how I want to live *my* life, Abbey,' he countered with dangerous calm. 'Are you sure this isn't about you and your own misgivings about parenthood?'

Abbey was appalled. 'I love children,' she defended herself hotly. 'But I'd prefer to have them when the time is right and with a man I love and who l-loves me. A man I can *rely* on!'

Nick recoiled as if she'd slapped him. For several moments he just sat there. Then with a savage yank he hauled his pen from his top pocket and added a bold signature to the prescription. 'There you are, Dr Jones.' He stood abruptly, as if to physically distance himself from what she'd asked him to do. Moving to the window, he reached out like a blind man towards the sill, gripping it with both hands, staring out.

Shakily, Abbey picked up the slip of paper. Her composure was shattering. 'I'm just trying to be responsible, Nick.' She fluttered the words accusingly at his back and left quietly.

Oh, God, why was his throat tightening like this? 'How could she *think* I wouldn't want a child?' he rasped under his breath. '*Our* child.' He pressed his fingers across his eyes, as if staving off pain. What the hell was last night about then? His gut wrenched. How dumb can you be, Tonnelli? Obviously their love-making hadn't stopped her world the way it had stopped his!

Abbey sat frozenly at her desk, her head buried in her hands. She felt sick to her stomach. Nothing she'd said to Nick had come out right. Remembering, she felt her heart lurch painfully. It had taken her under five minutes to completely destroy everything precious between them. *Everything.*

When her phone rang, she reached out groggily and picked it up. 'Yes, Meri.' Her voice came out cracked and she swallowed thickly.

'The Wilsons are here.' Meri kept her tone pitched confidentially low.

'Who?' Abbey tried to concentrate.

'Ryan and Natalie. They want their baby immunised.'

'Oh, I remember now.' Abbey massaged a hand across her forehead, as if to clear her thinking process. 'We could probably fit them some time today, couldn't we?'

'Actually, they wondered if you'd see them now. They're a bit edgy. I gather it's been quite a big decision for them.'

'Oh, OK…' Abbey's brow furrowed. 'Give me two minutes and then show them in.' She replaced the receiver slowly.

She'd have to pull herself together somehow. She had a full list of patients and the world could not be shut out indefinitely. As

Meri knocked and showed the Wilson family in, she whipped her prescription off the desk and into her top drawer. Before the day got much older, she'd have to find a minute to nip out to the chemist.

About eleven o'clock, Nick called through on her intercom. 'I thought you'd like to know, Jim Ferguson just called,' he said crisply. 'Stuart's surgery went well. He's in Recovery.'

Abbey felt relief rush through her. 'That's wonderful news. Thanks,' she added after a second, but he'd already hung up.

Somehow they managed to avoid each other for most of the day. Only once did she encounter Nick, when she'd gone out to Reception and he'd been seeing off a young couple with their toddler. A cute little boy with a thatch of dark curls.

The young mother was smiling disarmingly at Nick. 'Keiran was so good today. You must have a way with kids, Dr Tonnelli. Could we book to see you for his next shot?'

His mouth a tight line, Nick shook his head. 'Dr Jones will look after you, Mrs O'Connor.'

He looked up and stared mockingly at Abbey. 'I won't be here.'

Abbey turned on her heel and almost ran back to her room, the drum-heavy thud in her chest almost suffocating her. Damn! Sick with hurt and disillusionment, she stabbed the computer off and shaded her eyes.

All day long, she'd allowed herself to nurture the faintest hope that somehow she and Nick could put things back together. But he couldn't have made it more clear that it was over. *Over.* She blinked through a blur of tears. Oh, Nick, what have I done?

CHAPTER ELEVEN

How on earth were they to go on from here? How?

Abbey stretched her time in the surgery for as long as she could and then went across to the hospital. Pinning a bright smile on her face, she went through the motions, doing a ward round slowly and methodically.

Anything to delay going home. Except how could she think of it as home any longer? She and Nick would be stepping round each other like strangers. She bit her lips tightly together, smothering a bitter smile. The only time she'd fallen headlong in love in the whole of her life—and it had ended in disaster and heart-break.

There was no feeling of warmth in the house when she opened the back door. No comforting aroma of a meal being lovingly prepared.

But the lights were on so Nick must be home. Perhaps there was still hope…

Her breath caught and shuddered in her throat and her lips parted softly as she called, 'Nick?'

'In here.'

Abbey took a breath so deep it hurt, then on rubbery legs she made her way through the archway into the lounge. Nick was there, standing by the fireplace, his bags packed and set neatly against the wall beside him. Staring at him, the tight set to his mouth and jaw, Abbey felt her heart was splitting in two. She closed her eyes briefly and then forced herself to look at him. 'You're leaving.'

'There's no point in me staying.'

'But you came for a month!'

He made a rough sound of scorn. 'Just gives weight to your perception of my unreliability, then, doesn't it?'

'That wasn't what I meant to say!' She defended herself raggedly. 'It just came out that way…'

'The hell it did.' Pretending not to see the raw look of hurt on her face, he hardened his gaze even further. 'I wish I could say it's been worth it, Abbey, but we both know I'd be lying. I was an arrogant fool to have come here at all.' Their gazes locked for a long time, before he stooped and picked up his bags. 'I won't ask you to think of me sometimes,' he stated bitterly, and then he was gone, leaving her alone.

Except she wasn't alone.

The house was full of reminders of him. From the stoneware he'd bought to make his special lasagne to the bottles of wine he'd chosen so carefully and which they'd never opened.

Dull depression settled on her like a cloud, but resolutely she went through to her bedroom, stripping off the sheets and pillowcases and stuffing them into the washing machine.

And she'd be darned if she'd use this particular bed linen ever again—not with the scent of him still clinging to it and swathing her in a heartbreaking mist of remembering…

'Nick not coming in today?' It was the next morning and Meri had just put a mug of coffee on Abbey's desk.

'No…' Abbey sighed, daunted by the need for explanation. 'Actually, Meri…he's left Wingara.'

The two women stared awkwardly at each other, and then Meri took the initiative. 'I'm really sorry to hear that, Abbey. But I've been around the traps long enough to know neither of you would have made the decision lightly.'

Except the decision for him to leave hadn't been hers at all. 'Thanks, Meri.' Abbey's voice shook fractionally. 'We'll just have to soldier on, won't we?'

Meri looked wry. 'Women have been doing it since time began.'

The next month brought no relief to Abbey's pain and deep sense of loss. On the lighter side, the Frasers were home and quietly optimistic that Stuart would have no residual effects from his surgery.

'I'm just so happy to have him beside me at night,' Andrea confessed during a flying visit to Abbey for a pap smear. 'Just to hold each other. And if that's all we can have...' Her eyes misted over.

'Andi, it's early days yet.' Abbey swabbed the specimen onto a slide. 'And you said the specialist's last report was very encouraging. Let's just concentrate on things working out wonderfully for you and Stuart.'

'Amen to that.' Andrea settled herself back in the chair. 'Do you want to talk about what happened between you and Nick?' she asked with the easy frankness of friendship. 'You were so right for each other, Abbey.'

'Oh, please...' Abbey went to wash her hands. 'It didn't work out, Andi,' she said wearily. 'Can we leave it at that?'

Andrea bit her lip. 'You look awful, Abbey—so strained. Couldn't you...?' Andi waved her hands about helplessly.

'No.' Abbey's answer was unequivocal. 'I should have the results of your test back in a week,' she sidetracked professionally. 'I'll ring if there's anything untoward.'

Another month went by.

'Meri, I have to go to Hopeton next week.' Abbey pushed the desk diary aside and pocketed her ballpoint. 'Could you call Wolf and see if he's available to provide cover? I'll need Wednesday and Thursday.'

'Sure.' Meri made a note on her pad. 'Regional meetings again?'

'Mmm.' Amongst other things, Abbey thought sombrely.

'You have a visitor.' Meri was all smiles when Abbey arrived back during the late afternoon from her trip to Hopeton.

Abbey came to a halt, her lungs fighting for air. Was it Nick? Had he come back?

'Go on,' Meri insisted in her best managing voice. 'He's waiting in your office.' She reached out a hand and swept up the post. 'I'm just off. See you both in the morning.'

Afterwards, Abbey had no clear idea how her legs had carried her along the corridor to her office. Heart trampolining, she turned the knob and pushed the door slowly open. And gave a tiny gasp, as the tall male figure turned from the window.

'Steve!' She dropped her bag and ran into her brother's outstretched arms. And promptly burst into tears.

'Have you missed me that much, little sis?' Steve seemed amused.

'Must have, mustn't I?' With a watery smile, Abbey eased herself away.

He gave her an astute brotherly glance. 'Don't think so, Abbey. You look like you've just come from Heartbreak Hotel.'

Abbey sniffed and gave a funny little grimace. 'Very droll. Are you writing an agony column these days?'

'Not me.' He shook his fair head. 'But I know the signs, kiddo, and my doctoring instincts tell me my little sister is in need of some TLC. Come on.' He looped an arm around her shoulders. 'Let's get you home and fed.'

It was lovely to be cosseted. Tucked up on the sofa in the lounge room, Abbey sipped gratefully at the big mug of scalding tea, replete from the helping of fluffy scrambled eggs Steve had magically produced in record time.

Watching her fork up the meal hungrily, he'd demanded, 'Why aren't you eating properly?'

'I am.'

'Not from what I saw in the fridge.'

Abbey had shrugged uninterestedly. 'There's stuff in the freezer.'

She looked up now as he sauntered back into the room and asked, 'All squared away?'

'Yep.' He looked at her narrowly. 'More tea?'

'No, thanks. But that was lovely, Steve.' She leaned over to place her empty mug on the side table.

Steve seemed to hesitate and then, as if coming to a decision, bounded across to the sofa. 'Shove up a bit, hmm?' Obediently, Abbey drew her knees up and he plonked down beside her, his head resting on the cushioned back, his legs outstretched and crossed at the ankles. He glanced across at her. 'OK, let's have it, Abbey.'

Abbey sighed and closed her eyes. 'Do you have all night?'

'If necessary. Come on.' His hand covered hers, hard and strong. 'Roll it out. It's probably not half as bad as you think.'

Abbey swallowed and swallowed again and made a tentative beginning. 'There's a man...'

'Does this man have a name?'

'Nicholas Tonnelli.'

'Hell. How did you get hooked up with him?'

So she told her brother the whole sad story.

When she'd finished, Steve rolled his head across the cushioned back to look at her. 'So you're going to contact him, right?'

'How can I?' she said bleakly. 'He hates me.'

'Rats! How could he hate you? You've both got your wires crossed, that's all.'

If only it was that simple.

'You have to see Nick and talk to him, Abbey,' Steve repeated. 'Or I will.'

She snatched her hand back. 'Don't you dare! Keep out of it, Steve.'

'No, I won't. These are lives we're talking about here, Abbey, yours and—'

She let out a wail and he stopped and hugged her close. 'Come on, kid. You can do it. Remember the courage you found when Mum and Dad died? Through all the stuff we had to do?'

She met his eyes, her own troubled. 'It's not the same.'

'Yes, it is. Trust me, I'm a doctor.'

That old cliché brought a wobbly smile to her mouth. 'Will you come with me?'

'Uh-uh. But I'll hold the fort while you're gone.'

'How long are you down for?'

He lifted a shoulder. 'As long as I need. My contract's finished.'

Abbey perked up. 'So you're going to settle back in Australia?'

'Eventually. Actually...' He looked at the floor, faintly embarrassed. 'I've met a girl, Catherine. She's a surgeon.'

'And?' Abbey prodded him with her toe.

He looked sheepish. 'We, uh, got married.'

'Oh, my God! That's fantastic!' She took both his hands in hers, for the first time noticing his gold wedding band. 'So, what are you doing here? Why aren't you with your wife?'

'I came down to see you. To tell you about the marriage and take you back for a holiday with us. But I guess there's no chance of that now, is there?'

Abbey shook her head slowly, pushing a strand of hair back from her face. 'How long had you and Catherine known each other?'

'Couple of months. But we just knew it was right between us, Abbey. As right as it will be for you and Nick.'

If only she could believe that.

Steve insisted she take a few days off work and rest. 'I'll muddle along with Meri's help.

And I promise I won't kill off any of your patients. Well, not intentionally.' He grinned.

She gave him a shaky smile. 'Thanks, Steve. I owe you one.'

He reached out and cuffed her chin. 'Just be nice to Catherine when you meet her.'

'Of course I'll be nice to Catherine. When is she coming down?'

Steve made a face. 'As soon as she can. Her contract still has another few weeks to run. Hopefully, there'll be a suitable practice some- where we can invest in. We've managed to save a bit. But back to you,' he said softly. 'When are you going to see Nick?'

Abbey's stomach heaved alarmingly. 'You're not going to give up, are you?'

'Nope.'

'Day after tomorrow, then. I'll drive to Hopeton and get a flight to Sydney from there.' And pray to heaven Nick would see her.

Abbey had travelled barely thirty minutes from Wingara when her mobile phone rang. She rolled her eyes. It was probably Steve again, checking on her. He'd already rung once. Automatically, she reduced her speed and pulled her car to a stop. Activating the speak button, she put the phone to her ear. 'Hello.'

'Abbey, don't hang up!'

Abbey felt as though her heart had flown into her mouth. Her lungs, starved for air, felt crushed. For a second she feared she was about to pass out. 'Nick?'

'Yes. I'm on my way to Wingara to see you.'

'But I'm on my way to see *you*!' She heard his swift intake of breath. 'I've only just left town.'

'All right…' He seemed to be thinking. 'I'm about an hour away. Turn round and head back, Abbey. I'll meet you at home.'

Home. Abbey swallowed. Had she heard right?

'Abbey, did you get that?'

'Yes.' Silly tears clumped on her lashes and she swiped them away. 'I'll be waiting for you…'

Abbey leaned back on the headrest until she felt calm enough to restart the Range Rover. But first she should call Steve, she supposed, and tell him what had happened.

'So, I'll steer clear for the next day and a half, then, shall I?'

'Idiot brother.' But she was smiling.

Abbey had steeled herself for a great deal of awkwardness when they met, running over little speeches in her head. But the reality turned out to be very different from what she'd imagined.

Nick drove in slowly and parked around the back of the house. His heart was clamouring. Switching off the engine, he sat for a moment looking into space. Suddenly his hand clenched on the wheel, the sharp edge of need ripping through him. He swallowed against the sudden constriction in his throat. Just don't mess this up, Tonnelli, he cautioned himself silently. Or you'll lose her for ever.

And why was he still hanging about here? He threw open the door of the Jag and swung out.

And Abbey was standing there. Waiting.

'Hello,' she croaked.

'Hello, yourself.' Nick's gaze snapped over her. 'You've lost weight.'

'And you need a shave,' she told him candidly.

He smiled slightly, lifting a hand and scrubbing it over his jaw. 'I've been on the road since four o'clock this morning.'

'You've driven all the way from Sydney?'

'Yes, Abbey.' His eyes burned like emeralds. 'To ask you to marry me.'

'Oh.' Abbey thought she might have fallen in a heap if his arms had not gone around her, holding her as if he'd never let her go.

After a long time he pulled back, lifting his hands to bracket her face, his entire heart in his gaze. 'This feels so right, doesn't it? You and me?'

Abbey nodded, tears welling up and overflowing.

'Don't cry, sweetheart!' Nick took her hands and curled them over his heart. 'I love you!'

'Now he tells me…' Abbey hiccuped a laugh. 'After I've spent the loneliest weeks of my life.'

'It's been hell for me, too.' His voice shook. 'You should never have allowed me to walk out the way I did, Abbey.'

'How was I supposed to stop you?' flashed Abbey, dazed by the brush of his lips against hers. 'Let the air out of your tyres?'

'Might have worked.' Smiling, Nick felt the knot in his chest begin to unravel. It was going to be all right. His arms went around her again, wrapping her against him, his mouth claiming hers as if he was dying of thirst.

A whimper rose in her throat and, breaking the kiss, Nick scooped her into his arms and carried her inside to the lounge room, making a beeline for the sofa. He sat down, settling her on his knee. 'So, what's your answer, Abbey?' he asked softly, his throat working. 'Will you marry me?'

'Of course I'll marry you.' Shakily, she stretched out a hand, touching his hair, the outside edge of his ear, the soft hollow in his throat. 'But I don't want to put any pressure on you.'

He lifted his head and looked at her in puzzlement. 'How could you possibly do that?'

She looked into his eyes, reading the sincerity and, unmistakably, the love. Joy, clear and pure, streamed through her. She dropped her gaze shyly. 'I have to tell you something, Nick.'

'That you love me?' His voice was gentle.

'Of course that.' She burrowed closer. 'I— That is—we…' She hesitated and blinked rapidly.

'You've got me worried now, Abbey.' Nick gave her a little shake. 'Just tell me.'

'I'm pregnant.'

A beat of absolute silence.

'Pregnant!' Nick sat back hard in the sofa. 'You mean you didn't take the—?'

'No.' Abbey shook her head. 'It was such a terrible day and the patient list was endless.' She stopped and took a long shuddering breath. 'And by the time I realised I hadn't had the script filled, it was late and we'd had that awful fight. Well, I just wanted to die and—'

'Oh, Abbey. My poor sweet darling.' His arms went around her and he was rocking her. 'You should've thumped me. I behaved so selfishly, so ego-driven. But a baby?' His gaze clouded and he turned her head and looked into her eyes. 'Are you sure?'

'Yes.' She choked on a laugh. 'I've had it confirmed.'

'Whew!' Nick let the air out of his lungs in a long hiss. 'We're having a baby.'

'Are you pleased?' Abbey's voice was suddenly thin with unshed tears.

'Oh, God, yes!' His hand smoothed over her tummy, as though already he hoped to find there might be changes. 'Oh, this is something, isn't it? But how have you managed on your own?' A frown touched his eyes. 'Have you been sick?'

'A bit queasy,' she confessed with a grimace. 'But something wonderful happened.' Excitedly, she told him about her brother's unexpected arrival and the support he'd offered.

'Then thank heaven for Steve.' Nick held her more closely. 'I'd better buy him a beer.'

Abbey chuckled. 'He'll want several, I should think. And he's recently married.' She filled Nick in about Catherine.

'Good grief,' he grumbled. 'I leave the place for five minutes and all this happens.'

'Then you'd better stick close to me in future, hadn't you?' Abbey pressed her forehead against his.

'Depend on that.' Nick caught her hand and began kissing her fingers one by one. 'Will you mind living in Sydney?' His mouth twisted with faint irony. 'I don't think it would be practical for me to relocate here.'

Abbey wriggled closer. 'As long as we're together, I don't mind where we live.'

'But knowing you and how much you care about your patients, I imagine you'll want to find a replacement before we can make any firm wedding plans?'

'Actually…' She made a little moue of conjecture. 'It's just occurred to me Wingara might be the ideal set-up for Steve and Catherine.'

They smiled like a pair of conspirators and Nick raised a dark eyebrow. 'So we could get married soon, then?'

'Soonish. I'd like to wait for Catherine to be here.' Thoughtfully, Abbey ran her finger down the front of his shirt. 'I don't have much family…'

'Silly girl—of course you do,' he murmured unsteadily. 'You have me—and our baby.'

A slow, radiant smile lit her face. 'I do, don't I? I love you, Nicholas.'

His eyes closed and when he opened them, the message shone clear. 'And I love you, Abbey Jones.'

And the way he kissed her then convinced Abbey, as no words ever could, that he certainly did.

MEDICAL ROMANCE™

Large Print

Titles for the next six months…

February

THE PREGNANCY PROPOSITION   Meredith Webber
A WHITE KNIGHT IN ER   Jessica Matthews
THE SURGEON'S CHILD   Alison Roberts
DR MARCO'S BRIDE   Carol Wood

March

A VERY SPECIAL MARRIAGE   Jennifer Taylor
THE ELUSIVE CONSULTANT   Carol Marinelli
ENGLISHMAN AT DINGO CREEK   Lucy Clark
THE FRENCH SURGEON'S SECRET CHILD   Margaret Barker

April

THE BABY BONDING   Caroline Anderson
IN-FLIGHT EMERGENCY   Abigail Gordon
THE DOCTOR'S SECRET BABY   Judy Campbell
THE ITALIAN DOCTOR'S PROPOSAL   Kate Hardy

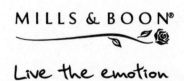

MILLS & BOON®

Live the emotion

0104 LP 2P P1 Medical

MEDICAL ROMANCE™

Large Print

May

OUTBACK ENGAGEMENT	Meredith Webber
THE PLAYBOY CONSULTANT	Maggie Kingsley
THE BABY EMERGENCY	Carol Marinelli
THE DOCTOR'S CHRISTMAS GIFT	Jennifer Taylor

June

FOR CHRISTMAS, FOR ALWAYS	Caroline Anderson
CONSULTANT IN CRISIS	Alison Roberts
A VERY SPECIAL CHRISTMAS	Jessica Matthews
THE ITALIAN'S PASSIONATE PROPOSAL	Sarah Morgan

July

OUTBACK MARRIAGE	Meredith Webber
THE BUSH DOCTOR'S CHALLENGE	Carol Marinelli
THE PREGNANT SURGEON	Jennifer Taylor
THE GP'S SECRET	Abigail Gordon

MILLS & BOON®

Live the emotion

0104 LP 2P P2 Medical